SCARS

For Jean, always.

And for every abuse survivor and every person
who's ever hurt themselves to cope
or felt so alone in their pain—
and for those who love and support us.
I hope you find safety, love, and happiness
—and the delight of a good story.

SCARS

Cheryl Rainfield

WestSide Books
Lodi, New Jersey

Published by WestSide Books
60 Industrial Road
Lodi, NJ 07644
973-458-0485
Fax: 973-458-5289

This is a work of fiction. All characters, places, and events
described are imaginary. Any resemblance to real people,
places, and events is entirely coincidental.

Library of Congress Cataloging-in-Publication Data

Rainfield, C. A. (Cheryl A.)
Scars / by Cheryl Rainfield. -- 1st ed.
p. cm.
Summary: Fifteen-year-old Kendra, a budding artist, has not felt safe since she began
to recall devastating memories of childhood sexual abuse, especially since she cannot
remember her abuser's identity, and she copes with the pressure by cutting herself.
ISBN 978-1-934813-32-4
[1. Sexual abuse--Fiction. 2. Emotional problems--Fiction. 3. Cutting (Self-mutilation)--Fiction. 4. Self-mutilation--Fiction. 5. Artists--Fiction. 6. Lesbians--Fiction.
7. Memory--Fiction.] I. Title.
PZ7.R1315Sc 2010
[Fic]--dc22

2009052076

International Standard Book Number: 978-1-934813-32-4
School ISBN: 978-1-934813-34-8
Paperback ISBN: 978-1-934813-57-7
Cover Photograph Copyright © by Stripped Media
Cover design by David Lemanowicz
Interior design by David Lemanowicz

Printed in the United States of America
10 9 8 7 6 5 4 3 2 1

First Edition

SCARS

1

"Someone is following me." I gulp air, trying to breathe.

Carolyn leans forward, her face worried. "What makes you say that?" There's a hesitation in her voice that stings me.

"You don't believe me!" I spit the words out at her, then look away, twisting my hands together to keep them from trembling.

"I didn't say that. I don't know enough about this yet to know what to believe. Why don't you tell me about it?"

So you can go tell my parents?

But she won't; I know she won't. Client-therapist confidentiality, and all that. And I trust Carolyn; I really do. But does she trust me?

I run my tongue over my dry lips. It almost doesn't seem real, now that I'm sitting here in her air-conditioned office. *But I didn't imagine it. I couldn't have.*

"I hear footsteps behind me when I'm out walking alone. Heavy footsteps that stop when I stop, and start when I start."

Carolyn nods, her gaze never leaving mine, and I know she's taking me seriously.

My breath is so shallow I'm almost dizzy. "I keep looking back, but I never see anyone watching me. But as soon as I start walking again, the footsteps are there."

I know how that sounds. Like I'm paranoid. Crazy. I'm so afraid I'm imagining all of this, that it's just an echo from the past. But that doesn't make the watched feeling go away. It's only gotten stronger.

I look out the window, away from Carolyn's worried eyes, and stare at the buildings across from us, at the dirty red bricks, the storefront windows, the parking signs shaking in the wind. My arm throbs with pain beneath my long sleeve.

I usually feel so safe in Carolyn's office, but nothing is working today—not the soft green ferns on her bookshelves, not the smell of peppermint tea and honey, not even the soothing sound of her voice. If I could draw her office right now, I'd use the dark, heavy lines of charcoal and the foggy greyness of an ink wash, not the bright, happy colors of gouache that I usually see here.

I shiver. "I heard the footsteps again this morning—but I was too scared to turn around."

"That sounds terrifying." Carolyn crosses her legs. "But have you thought of the possibility that someone was just going the same way as you?"

"It didn't feel like that…" I'm shaking now, trembles coming from deep inside me, spreading outward. "Do you believe me?" I feel like a little kid looking for reassurance, not a fifteen-year-old who's in the top ten of her class.

Carolyn looks at me with so much compassion that I want to bolt from the room. I want to accept her caring, to just gather it in, but I'm afraid to. I'm afraid of how much I need it—and how much it'll hurt if she stops.

Carolyn touches my hand, her wedding ring as warm as her skin. "I believe you, Kendra."

"You do?" My shaking stops.

"I do. You've never given me any reason to doubt you."

But having no reason to doubt me is not the same as believing me. The shaking starts up again.

"Do you have any idea of who it might be?" Carolyn's voice is soft, like she knows I want to run.

A door snapping shut. His hand on my wrist.

"It's. . . .*him*."

"The man who molested you?"

"Yes." I wince and clench my trembling hands in my lap, digging my nails into my palms. But the trifling pain isn't enough to distract me.

"It must be terrifying for you to think he's out there somewhere."

"It is," I whisper.

"But Kendra, pedophiles don't usually come after their victims, especially not years later. They like easy access and frightened, compliant children who they can manipulate—not active teen girls who might fight back."

"I know. But—" I glance at my sleeve, make sure the white bandage isn't poking through. "I just have this feeling—this gut sense—that it's *him*."

Carolyn looks at me steadily. "And your intuition is more finely tuned than most people's. It had to be, for you to survive."

I shrug, but I know she's right.

A door snapping shut. His hand gripping my wrist. A handkerchief falling. I squeeze my fist; the stiff skin beneath my bandage screeches, spreading pain through my whole body. I clench my jaw and breathe out slowly. *Can't let the pain show.*

"What're you thinking right now?" she asks.

"Nothing!" I squeeze harder, hoping the pain will clear my head.

"It looks to me like something's going on."

I don't know how she knows when something's wrong, but she always does. I've got to tell her something, anything just to keep her away from my arm. *His hand, gripping my wrist. His breath against my cheek.* "I've got to remember who he is."

"That will come when you're ready."

But what if I'm never ready? What if he gets me first?

"Do you want to explore your memories? We have time."

"I will kill you if you tell."

"No!"

I snatch my backpack off the ground and rummage through it, looking for my sketches, my doodles, for anything I can use to distract her—to distract us both.

"I mean—I don't think I'm ready." *But I have to be. I have to figure out who he is. So why do I feel like I'm going to vomit when I think about it?*

I yank things out of my backpack—a bruised apple, an English test, an overdue library book, but no sketchbook. I dump my backpack upside down; pens, pencils, my dirty gym socks, a half-eaten granola bar all fall out. I shake my bag harder. Then a bright square of paper falls out.

It's a deep magenta, almost red, folded into stiff squares. I've never seen it before. I pick it up by its shiny edges and open it. It makes a crackling sound.

There are only a few words typed on the page, but they cut through me like a blade: *"You have broken your promise."*

My breath shudders in my throat. *His hand gripping my wrist. His lips against my ear.*

"What is it?" Carolyn asks, from far away.

I hand her the note with unsteady hands. "It's from *him.*"

2

I get up and pace the length of the room, my vision blurring. I can't believe this is happening. But in some corner of my heart, I've been waiting for him to hurt me, the way he said he would. All these years, I've been waiting for him to silence me.

I glance at the note, and I'm almost glad this is happening. It's proof that I'm not making it all up—that someone really *is* following me.

Carolyn smooths out the note. "This is cryptic, maybe even menacing. But are you sure it isn't from a classmate? Some student pulling a prank?"

I stop pacing and stare down at the rug, losing myself in the pattern. I want her to be right, for it to be just some jerk trying to crank me up. But my gut says it's *him*.

My thoughts keep jaggedly circling back to the knowledge that he is after me. Even though I've been waiting for something bad to happen, now that it's actually happening, I'm not ready for it. I don't know what to do.

I force myself to look up. "I'm sure. Pretty sure, anway. It feels like something he'd say."

"Well, if it really is your abuser, then he's sending you a very clear message." Carolyn sets the note down on the table, next to her date book. "Do you want me to contact the police?"

"I will kill you if you tell."

"No!"

"Are you sure, Kendra?"

"I'm sure." *He* put that paper in my backpack. He *knows* how to find me. I can't give him a reason to come after me. "I don't see what good it would do. Besides, I've almost got him." I take a deep, shuddering breath. "He had access to my backpack. That means he must be a teacher at school or someone from art class, or . . ."

Or Sandy. I feel sick. I had my backpack with me last night when I went over to visit him. I thought he was just being a mother hen when he looked at me with that worried frown he gets between his eyebrows and said I could talk to him about anything. But now I wonder if he was trying to get me to tell him what I remember—to betray myself.

I push my breath out. It *can't* be Sandy. If it was him, would he really have pushed me to talk after he saw my drawing of rape? Would he really have called the police? Unless that was just a clever way to keep me from suspecting him...

No. Sandy's too gentle to do anything like what I've remembered. It's *not* him.

The sick feeling subsides.

Carolyn glances at the heap of stuff that came out of my backpack. "How often do you empty your knapsack like that?"

"I don't know. Every few months, I guess." My legs grow weak. I sink onto the couch. "You think the note's been there that long?"

"It may have been. What do you think?"

"I think I'm no closer to finding out who he is."

Carolyn tilts her head, the look in her eyes intense. "The answer is there, inside you."

I sigh. I know she's right. The memories are so strong, all I have to do is close my eyes and reach for them and they come. I'm the one who keeps trying to hold them back. I'm the one who wants to run screaming from my own head. "Okay, I'll try to listen. But would you sit with me?"

"Of course." Carolyn comes over and sits down beside me on the couch.

I take her hand. It's solid, warm and reassuring.

"You can stop any time you want," she says.

I close my eyes and sink into the darkness. Almost before I can take a breath, I feel *him* in front of me, his hands gripping my wrists, holding me still.

I want to cry out, to open my eyes and bring myself back, but I know I've got to stay here, my breath caught in my throat, until I can see his face. Until I know who *he* is.

"Where are you, Kendra? Tell me what you see."

I force myself to look. "A hardwood floor. Black shoes. My underwear in a crumpled ball." I'm shuddering now, great heaving shudders that shake my whole body.

"I'm right here with you, Kendra," Carolyn says. She squeezes my hand, and I know that I can find my way back through the shadows if I need to.

I take a breath, then another. I raise my gaze higher. "I

14

see . . . his open belt. His big hands. His unbuttoned shirt and curly hair on his chest."

I'm so close to seeing his face now. I clench my hands together—I'm really going to get there! I force my gaze up to the creases in his neck—and then everything stops: all sound, color, breathing—frozen like a still life. My chest aches with the breath caught inside me; I can't feel my hand touching Carolyn's, can't feel the couch beneath me.

"I will kill you," he hisses. "I will kill you if you tell."

"I won't tell. I promise I won't."

He releases my wrist.

My breath returns, and along with it come color and sound. I feel air rush into my lungs. See Carolyn's worried eyes. Feel her hand clasping mine.

"What happened?" she says. "What did you see?"

"I saw . . . nothing."

I don't think she believes me. But I can't tell her how close I came to seeing his face. Can't tell her how easy it would be to see it with her beside me, keeping me safe. Because I wouldn't be safe for long. Not when he's after me. Not if he found out what I'd remembered.

Panic rises inside me, flattening my lungs, and I want to cut myself until the fear is gone. I can almost feel the utility knife in my hand: its narrow plastic handle; its ridges on the edge; the button to push the blade up. I can almost smell the bitter odor of metal and blood.

I turn my face away from Carolyn and try to keep my breathing steady. If I had my knife right now, I'd go into the bathroom, lock myself in a stall, and cut my arm until I could breathe again, until all the ugly pictures were gone.

But I don't have my knife with me. And even if I did, I couldn't run out like that. Because I can't let Carolyn know. I can't let *anyone* know.

I've managed to hide the cutting for six months, ever since the memories started. Six whole months, and I can hide it for six more—or however long it takes to get through this. Because I know people wouldn't understand. They'd try to take it from me. And I need it. I need it to keep going.

Carolyn leans closer, and I know she's trying to see my face. "How are you feeling, Kendra?"

I blink. *Got to be careful. Got to keep her away from my arm.* I turn to face her and lick my lips. "Scared, I guess."

"That's probably how you felt when he hurt you, isn't it? Scared. But it's rare for a pedophile to go after his victim. They prefer to use coercion and threats to keep their victims quiet."

Somehow that doesn't make me feel any better. Besides, I don't think this guy fits the profile. He's already risked exposing himself by following me and by putting the note in my bag. How much harder would it be for him to hurt me?

I want to cut so badly, I ache with the need for release. I turn away from Carolyn and pump my fist hard, feeling the scabs tear apart, feeling the dull, aching pain—but it's not enough. Not anywhere near enough.

His hands, squeezing my throat. Blackness edging into my eyes.

It's hard to keep sitting here, to keep from running out of the room. I want to slice open my flesh, feel the panic drain away with my blood, but I can't—not in front of Carolyn. Not in front of anyone.

"What can we do to help you right now?" Carolyn asks. "Can you imagine your fear as an object or a color and take a step back from it?"

I listen to her soothing voice and feel the shadows pull back. I feel myself relax. My need to cut lessens, and I breathe slower. And then the session is over.

I'm not ready to go yet. It's days and days till I see her again.

I wish I could see her more often. I wish she was my mother.

I push the thought away. I've got a mother. But Carolyn—she gets me on a level no one else does. And she gives me more comfort and caring in one session than my mother ever has in my whole life, even if I added it all together.

Pain tinges the comfort I was starting to feel. I pick things up off the floor slowly and shove them back in my bag.

Carolyn walks over to the windowsill and comes back with her basket of shells and stones—ridged shells with traces of pink and orange and brown at their tips and polished gemstones with swirls of color running through them. "Would you like to take one of these with you? To remind you that I'm here and that I'm thinking about you?"

I swear she can read my mind. I smile a little and root through the stones, picking one that feels heavy and right in my hand, a stone with brown and gold streaks, like her hair. "Thank you."

"You take care, now."

The magenta note is there on her desk, like a square of bloody paper. Screams start up inside me again. I turn, then escape down the stairs and out onto the street, the cool morning air brushing against my face.

My back prickles, like someone's watching me. I whirl around. All I see are people on their way to work, kids on their way to school—no one who's paying attention to me.

Maybe I really am making it all up.

No. That note was real. He left me that note.

I run the rest of the way to school.

3

I walk down the crowded hall to my locker. *I wish I didn't have to be here. What does biology or algebra or sonnets have to do with anything I'm going through?*

I turn the combination on my lock and wrench the door open. I'm shaking inside, a trembling that won't stop. I wish I'd brought my utility knife with me, but I didn't think I'd need to cut. Not at school.

The constant noise makes me want to scream—people slamming their lockers shut, girls giggling with each other, sneakers squeaking down the hall, boys burping as loud as they can—but I know I'm only feeling like this because of the note.

And I can't let myself think about that.

My arm is hot and stiff, every jostle sending pain through me. But it's not the bright, hard pain that makes everything go away. It's an annoying, irritating pain that makes me grit my teeth. I wish I could tear my nails through my flesh like blades. I don't know if I can go through the whole day without finding a way to cut.

I ram my books into my backpack and slam my locker shut. Sarah's locker, beside mine, is still empty. My throat tightens, and I have to turn away. I miss her like an ache inside me, even though it's been five months, even though I should have gotten over her by now. I want to kick her locker in, smash it until it's flat, but that won't bring her back.

Everyone seems to have a group they belong to or at least someone they hang out with. When Sarah was here, we would walk the halls together, two of the smart kids that nobody hassled—mostly because Sarah could talk to anyone and make them feel special. Now I stand out like a giant pimple on a chin.

I notice there's a strange lull in the noise. I look up to see Danny and Kirk heading down the hall—two big, solid lugs who like pushing people around.

I look away, but Danny's caught my gaze and is steering toward me.

"Got a problem?" he asks loudly.

No problem, except having you in my face.

Danny hooks his thumbs into his belt as he steps closer. I can't look away. I know I should move, but it's like I'm caught in a time warp. *I'm six again, and he's coming toward me, his belt undone. His breath is on my cheek.*

No. It's Danny's breath. He grips my face in his hand.

"Get away from me!" I screech, pushing at his chest, but he's like a wall, blocking off my world.

Then a body rams between us, a soft body that smells of musky amber and cigarettes, breaking Danny's hold and pushing me back against the lockers. I breathe in deeply, shudderingly as I flatten myself against the lockers. My rescuer is a girl I've seen around school—Meghan Ellis.

She's wearing a short leather skirt that shows off her butt, a white lacy bra, and not much else. There's a bright streak of blue in her long honey hair, and a flash of silver on her fingers. I recognize her because she's always getting into trouble—for talking back, for sitting down for the national anthem, and for punching out kids who bug her. That, and she sleeps around a lot.

They're circling each other like prizefighters, stopping in front of me.

"You don't own this school, Danny," Meghan says, tapping his chest with her finger, "so back off."

"Yeah? What's it to you?" Danny's huge shoulders bunch up, the veins in his neck pulsing. "You sleeping with girls now?"

My body flushes cold, then hot, as the hallway rings with laughter.

Pow! goes Meghan's fist, moving so fast that I almost don't see it jabbing Danny in the gut. And then he's twisting her arm back so far, it looks like it's going to snap.

Meghan grunts. I bite my lip hard enough to taste salty blood, and I inch backward. A combination lock's digging into my back.

"Nobody talks to me like that," Danny says. "Say you're sorry."

Meghan bares her teeth. "I just *did* talk to you like that, lover boy."

Danny jerks her arm back harder. I wish I had Sarah's ability to reason with people—or at least the courage to fight—but I just stand there, praying something will happen.

"Say it," Danny says.

Meghan shakes her head.

The pain is bad; I can see it in her face, in the way the skin around her eyes gets tight and her lips draw back in a hiss. I take a step sideways, then another; my hands sliding along the slick surface of the painted brick, searching for the fire alarm I know is there. *Come on!* Finally I feel the cold, protruding metal and grab the handle, pulling it down hard. Then I quickly jerk my hand away.

The fire alarm clangs madly. It's all chaos now, students erupting from classrooms and pouring into the hall, and teachers herding everyone toward the exits. Danny lets Meghan go, and then he and Kirk are swallowed up by the crowd.

I move closer to Meghan, who looks like she's trying hard not to cry. "Are you okay?"

She puts her hand on her hip. "'Course I am. Hey, you're not the scared little rabbit I thought you were." She blows the hair out of her eyes. "Thanks for saving my ass."

"*You're* the one who saved mine."

"Whatever." She grins. "Don't worry; I'm not going to let Danny get away with this."

"What do you mean?"

"Girls, get a move on," Mr. Blair shouts from behind us. "This is a fire alarm, not a gab session."

It *would* have to be him. I don't see why I have to go to school where one of Dad's friends works. He comes up behind me, practically breathing down my neck. I can smell

22

his sour coffee breath, sour like the man's. I stiffen. Is it *him*? He's known me long enough.

I leap away from him and rush through the doors and down the steps. When I look back, Mr. Blair is watching me, a grim expression on his face.

4

The fire alarm goes off again in second period—to great cheers from the students. I smell smoke even before I'm out of the classroom.

Everyone jostles each other, trying to get out first. I keep my body tight, away from the others. I can't stand feeling trapped.

I burst out into the hall and see Danny standing at his locker, its door open, flames licking up toward the ceiling. Thick black smoke is pouring out from the bottom, catching in my lungs and making my eyes water. I slip out of the rush of people and duck back against the wall, coughing. Danny howls something about his gym shorts.

Between the stampeding students, I catch glimpses of Meghan leaning against the lockers, chomping on her gum and watching Danny. She sees me and nods.

"Move along, folks," someone shouts.

I turn to see Mr. Blair striding towards us with a fire extinguisher. *Why couldn't it be any other teacher? Anyone but him.*

Mr. Blair frowns when he sees me, then turns his attention to Meghan. His gaze darts back and forth between her and Danny.

He knows; I'm sure of it. I dash through the crowd and grab Meghan's arm. "Come on!"

"No way. This is too good to miss."

I can hardly hear her over the insistent clanging of the fire alarm. I lean close. "Mr. Blair's watching you. And I think he knows."

Meghan shrugs. "So I miss school again. No biggie. But thanks for the tip."

Behind us, I hear the whoosh of the fire extinguisher. Meghan's smiling, but her eyes aren't; they're sad and old, the way I often feel. For a moment, it's like there's no distance between us. Then Meghan shakes her hair into her eyes and the connection breaks.

"If we leave now, he might forget about you," I say.

Meghan shrugs, the sadness back in her eyes. "I don't care. I'm trying to see how many times I can go to detention before my mom detaches her face from her beer can."

"I'm sorry." I touch her arm, but her face is closing up, her eyes masking over.

"Forget it. Just forget I said anything, okay?" She crosses her arms over her chest and turns to look at Mr. Blair. And I see her like a painting in my mind—a narrow, lonely figure leaning up against dented grey lockers, her face defiant yet vulnerable, the sadness trapped inside her.

But I wouldn't paint it like that. I'd paint her bandaged and bleeding, stumbling alone over the rubble of the hall, sharp slabs of the floor poking up to block her way, with smoldering lockers lying across her path—and nothing visible at the end of the smoke-filled hall.

25

Meghan doesn't look back at me. I know she wants me to leave. And some part of me understands; we both know how to hurt ourselves.

I turn and walk away.

❋

After the bell rings again, signaling all clear, I'm one of the first to get back into the school. Danny's locker is a sodden, blackened mess, and Meghan is nowhere to be seen. The art room is empty, with knapsacks and books scattered on the floor and tables, and art projects left undone.

The familiar smell of paint and clay rises up around me and I breathe it in deeply. It reminds me of afternoons with Sandy, of him working on his pottery wheel while I sat in the corner with crayons or a lump of clay or later on, with paints. Lightness fills my chest as I gather my paints, brushes, and paper.

And then I see the X-acto knives lying there, their sharp short blades like daggers rising from their handles. It's like they were left out just for me. I grab one, telling myself I'm only borrowing it for a few hours.

It would be so easy to cut, to just push my sleeve up, peel off the bandage, and cut—but I could never risk it, not where someone might see me. It almost feels like enough, just holding the knife, feeling its weight, the roughness of the etched metal handle, knowing I can cut if I need to. I tuck it into my bag between the pages of my sketchbook, then head to my table, the scent of paint and brushes already stirring images in my mind.

Students straggle into class, some grabbing their stuff and leaving, others sitting down to work. Mrs. Archer rushes in, her cheeks flushed, her copper hair shining. She winks at me from across the room, and I wish, as I always do, that she was my mother. I smile inside, but I ache, too. If I could put her and Carolyn together, I'd have the perfect mom—someone who understands my art, someone who understands my soul—and both of them like me just the way I am. But I know it's stupid to even think about.

Mrs. Archer bends over a student's work, and I twirl my paintbrush in my hand. If I were to paint her, I'd paint the warmth in her eyes, the brightness of her smile, and the way her nose crinkles up when she laughs. I'd paint the way her eyes take a person in, understanding and accepting everything and encouraging more. And I'd paint a tiny, inch-high figure of me, curled up in her and Carolyn's outstretched hands. But I haven't dared to paint either of them yet. It would make what I feel too real.

I dip my brush into the gouache, coating just the tip. The thick, opaque color clings to the bristles. Maybe I'll paint Carolyn and Mrs. Archer today. Maybe I'm ready. But when I put my brush to paper, it's Meghan who appears in the swirls of crimson, orange, and black. Pain flows from my fingertips and onto the paper, spreading before me like blood. The painting comes easily, like it's been waiting for me. A quick stroke of crimson here, a dab of black there, and then I'm done. I straighten up. The heavy ache inside me has gone.

I rinse my brush, then touch the soft, cool tips of the bristles to my lips. It feels comforting and somehow soothing. I need painting almost as much as I need cutting maybe more. Because if I couldn't paint, I'd be a girl without a mouth. I say things through painting that I can't say any other way. It's how I pull up hidden truths, express the pain that I hide from others. But when things are really bad, it's only my utility knife that releases the screams inside me.

Mrs. Archer leans over my work. "Wow. I like this," she says, tracing the dark, harsh lines of the figure. I've painted a girl, eyes huge and hurt, holding a flame out toward the darkness—only the flame is licking back to catch her hair.

"I like your use of symbolism here," she says. "It's very dark—but very strong. And your use of color is startling, yet pleasing. This is a piece to be proud of."

For a moment, I see my painting the way she does, with its beauty and strength. And then I start taking it apart, noticing the hand that's out of proportion, the shadows that are too deep. Mom would point all that out, telling me how stark and depressing it is or how the lack of color puts people off. And Dad would just say it's beautiful; he says that about all my art.

I look at my painting again and see how awkward it really is.

I slump against the table, holding my head in my hands.

"I'd like to display this, if I could," Mrs. Archer says. "Maybe it'll inspire some of my other students to paint like you."

I hunch away from her words. "You want them to paint things that scare people?" I force a laugh.

28

"No, Kendra. I want them to paint from the gut, where the real power is."

I can't laugh that one away. I know that's what I do.

I sit up straighter. "Thanks, but I'd like to keep this one."

Mrs. Archer pats the tabletop. "I understand."

But I'm not sure I do.

5

I look around for Meghan in the cafeteria, but I don't see her anywhere. I feel disappointed, almost angry—as if we'd planned to get together. But girls like Meghan don't mix with girls like me.

I sit down at the table where Sarah and I always sat, then take out my lunch and sketchbook, touching the X-acto knife beneath it for reassurance. There's a group of girls at the other end, all talking and laughing. But they won't bother me. They never do. Bothering me would mean having to acknowledge me, and they're way too cool for that.

I sharpen my pencils and press a 4B against the page, enjoying its soft darkness. I sketch as I eat, Meghan's face appearing on the page. I can't stop thinking about how beautiful she is—and how sad. She looks like a model, with natural highlights in her brown hair, a great body, and intense green eyes. And she knows it; I can tell by the way she tosses her hair over her shoulders, pouts her lips, and wears revealing clothes. I wonder if it bothers her, the way guys fall all over her, only looking at her body and not at what's in her eyes. Maybe all their attention helps her forget her sadness for a while. Or maybe it makes her feel more alone.

I watch for her the rest of the day, but I don't see her again. I wonder if the principal has sent her home to her drunken mother, if he even knows what she faces at home.

When the last bell rings, I walk the halls, looking for anyone who might be friends with her. She mostly hangs out with boys, if she hangs out with anyone at all.

I spot one: Jerry Farnsworth—tall, blond, and cute. A year older than we are. I swallow down my nervousness and walk up to him. "You know Meghan Ellis, right?" My voice squeaks.

"Who wants to know?" Jerry looks down at me. His smooth, tanned face is so handsome it's almost pretty, and he's wearing designer jeans and a dress shirt. A lot of girls in this school would love to have a reason to talk to him—but all I want to do is run away.

I wipe the sweat off my upper lip and blow the hair out of my face. "I just want to know where her locker is."

Jerry zips up his backpack and looks at me with his sky blue eyes. "You're not one of those bitches out to get Meghan, are you?"

I stare at him, not sure I've heard him right. The words don't seem to fit his handsome face.

Jerry closes his locker and turns to face me, his arms crossed over his chest. "Are you one of those catty types who makes life hell for Meg, or not?" He squints at me. "You don't really look the type."

Right. I'm not one of the beautiful people. Cute,

maybe, but not the obsessed-with-my-looks, caught-up-in-social-status type.

"No—I just want to be her friend," I say. I sound like I'm in second grade.

Jerry smiles like he finds me funny. "First locker after the science lab—208."

"Thanks." I turn to go.

"Hold on a sec." Jerry catches me by my arm. His gaze moves down my body slowly, pausing at my breasts.

Heat sweeps through me, blazing in my face. I wonder if he's looking at me like that because he knows what the man did to me. Maybe it's something boys can pick up on, the way a dog can smell when another dog is in heat. Jerry leans forward suddenly, smelling like tuna fish, and presses his open lips against mine. They're thick and rubbery, and they make me want to gag.

I shove him away, and then I'm running as fast as I can. I don't know if the laughter in my head is Jerry's or *his*.

I want to cut again, but I can't do it here. I stuff a note into Meghan's locker and then head for home. The closer I get, the slower my steps become, and the heavier my body feels. It's as if each step releases sedatives into my bloodstream. When I get to our street, I can see Mom standing in the doorway, ready to greet me like a social worker at a new job. Ever since she found out about the abuse, it's been her new role in life. It's like she thinks that if only she'd given me more attention, the abuse never would've happened. And who knows? Maybe she's right.

I clench my teeth, swallow down all the words that

want to fly out of me like hornets to sting her. *It's too late to fix things, Mom! Where were you, anyway, when he was raping me? Why didn't you protect me?* I reach the door, and Mom swings it open wide, the smell of turpentine and oil paint slapping my face.

I can't meet her eyes. She's interrupted work for me—again. "Don't bother me when I'm painting" is the law in our house. It makes me feel like I don't matter; I used to imagine screaming to get Mom's attention. I'm getting it now—not because of me, but because of what happened to me. And it feels all wrong.

I edge past her into the living room. She follows me so closely that she bumps into me when I stop.

"How was your day?" she asks in a fake-cheerful voice.

I shrug. *Why don't you just leave me alone? You don't really want to know how I feel.*

"Kendra?" Mom comes around and peers at me, a tremble creeping into her smiling mouth. *Like she actually cares, after all these years of not asking.*

"It was fine," I say in a clipped voice.

"Oh."

She looks away. I know she's disappointed. I'm not fake-happy enough. Not chatty and smile-even-if-you're-dying the way she is. I look past her and notice her painting propped up on the easel, glistening wet. Another forest scene. Technically perfect, with tiny, controlled strokes, as exact as a photo. But it feels empty to me, like there's no one behind the paintbrush. No emotion. Like a computer-generated image.

"I made a snack for you," Mom says, motioning toward the table.

Tofu dip and carrot sticks. *Woo–hoo.* "Thanks." I pick up a carrot and bite into it. It tastes like turpentine.

"Sandy called again." Her voice rises. "He said he had more books for you."

He can't have told her what the books are about. He wouldn't. "I'll pick them up later."

"I don't want you going over to his house too often."

"Why not?"

She gets a strange look on her face, almost as if she's mad at me. "Because he's a grown man. And because . . . I worry about you."

"You don't need to worry, Mom." *The worst has already happened.* "Sandy wouldn't hurt me. You should know; he's your friend, too!"

"A friend who's a man. And he's—you know—*gay.*"

Got a little hidden prejudice there? Man, what would you do if you knew about me?

"Why does he want you around, anyway? It's not natural."

You mean you can't figure out why someone likes me. "Just because he's gay doesn't mean he can't be friends with a girl."

Mom grimaces, as if my words make her smell something sour—like vomit. I don't think she knows how bad she looks when she does that; if she did, she wouldn't do it.

I pretend I don't see. "It's pretty common for gay men to have women friends."

"Women friends. Not girls."

Her face looks so different from her usual smooth mask. My fingers itch to get it down on paper—a thin charcoal smudge for the curl of her lips, burnt umber to emphasize the deep lines of her face, a sepia wash for the rest . . . .

"You have to be careful around men, honey. I'd think you, of all people, would know that."

"What's that supposed to mean?" I clench my fists so hard, the scabs rip open again.

Mom's hands flutter. "I don't think you should be alone with him. You know how men are . . . . "

"God, you're the one who used to take me over there when I was little! Besides, he's a decent guy. He wouldn't hurt me like that." *He can't have; I like him too much.*

"Well, I want you to be careful. Let me know when you leave. And don't stay too long. Really, that's just good manners." Her expression softens. "I care about you, Kendra, whether you believe it or not."

"I know you do." *But not the way I need you to.* I try not to choke on the stench of oil and turpentine. "Your painting is good, Mom."

"Your father thinks so, too." She looks at me with that funny expression again. "He says he likes watching me paint; I remind him of the girl he fell in love with."

Oh gag. I don't know what to say. "Well, I've got a lot of homework—"

"Your father thinks it's strange that you're not painting any more. We both do. He's worried about you."

"I'm *fine*," I say.

"Oh, honey, I wish you'd let me teach you again. You were showing such improvement!"

I keep my voice level and steady, though I feel like screaming. "I'm not ready to paint."

"But you were always so happy when you painted. Re-member?"

No. I was happy before you started telling me every-thing I was doing wrong. It's funny how you glide right over that, like Carolyn never got you to back off.

I glare at her neat rows of paints and brushes, all lined up on the dining room table according to color, size, and type. I could never work like that—so rigidly.

"Honey, don't let what you went through color your entire world. Don't let it make you give up painting."

I'm not giving it up, I almost say, but I stop myself, just in time. "I still love art. That hasn't changed."

"Appreciating art is not the same thing as creating it!"

"Can we just drop it?"

"Of course." But she smiles too brightly, and I know I've hurt her.

"I'm still an artist," I say.

Her eyes glisten. "I know you are."

I squirm, the truth pinching at me. But I know if I show her my paintings, she'll critique the joy right out of them, the way she did with my oils. And then what'll I have left?

Mom straightens the collar of my blouse. "How was your session with Carolyn?"

My heart pounds in my ears. I can't talk about the abuse. And I don't want to share Carolyn with her. Carolyn's the one good thing that Mom can't touch. "It went fine."

Mom yanks her hands away. "You never talk to me any more."

When did we ever talk? I have to stop myself from rolling my eyes. "I talk," I say.

"You don't. You never let me in."

"You never listen! You're always off doing something else."

"Well, I'm listening now. Come on, Kendra, how hard can it be?"

Too hard. I swallow. I know she's trying. I thought that's what I wanted, but I never imagined it would be like this. I rub my fingers against the bumpy white wall. Little bits of plaster rain to the floor, and Mom frowns. "I talked about *him*, okay? That's all I ever talk about."

"And? Did it help?"

You mean, did you get your money's worth? "That's not the way it works, Mom. I mean, yeah, it helped, but it's more something that happens over time, you know?" *But she doesn't know; I can see that.*

She twists her ring around her finger. "I wanted to talk to you about that."

I brace myself for whatever's coming.

"Your father and I—we'd like you to cut back on your sessions, maybe work towards ending them."

Pain lodges in my chest like a shard of metal. "What?"

"I know it isn't ideal," Mom says. "But money is going

to be tight around here for a while, and your therapy is one of the things that can go. We think you're mature enough that you can handle it."

"But I only just started!"

"I know it feels that way, honey, but it's been five months. And you seem to be doing so much better. You didn't think you were going to go forever, did you?"

I dig my nails into my palm. I want to cut so bad I can almost feel the sharp pain of the knife on my flesh, can almost feel the blood flowing—and then the relief. But my utility knife is in my desk drawer, forty steps away. Too far.

Mom is still talking; sound is pouring out of her mouth, but I only hear disconnected words. "Your father . . . downsizing . . . part-time job . . . can't pay our bills."

I'm watching her lips move, her forehead wrinkle as she frowns. But I'm so far away, she can't reach me. She doesn't even know I've left.

She's scared. I know that. I can see it in the tightness of her mouth, in the way her hands jerk as she talks. There's no way Mom can support us all on what she makes.

"He'll get another job, Mom. It'll be okay."

I can't believe I just did that. I did a Mom thing: saying everything will be okay when I don't see how it can be. But she seems to need it. To want it.

"You're right." Mom flashes me that plastic smile that she uses on gallery managers. "It'll all work out. And maybe you won't have to quit therapy."

But I can hear in her voice that she doesn't believe it.

"I can get a job, pay for my own sessions," I say, my voice high and thready.

"Not while you're in school, you can't," Mom says. "Your schoolwork is more important."

Schoolwork doesn't keep me alive. I fake a smile and edge out of the room.

"Where are you going?"

"Homework. I just—I can't do this right now, okay?"

No therapy. No Carolyn. No one to pull me out of the quicksand. I run down the hall before she can answer, my knapsack thunking like a fist into my back. I slam my door shut and ram my chair under the handle. I snatch up my utility knife and cut, fast and hard.

7

I don't feel anything at first: no relief, no comfort. Just the panic coiling inside me, vibrating in my chest. I slash again and again, flesh opening up to expose little white bubbles of fat, until dark blood wells up to cover them and spills over my arm in wide, curling arcs, thin and hot. I barely feel the pain—just the air rushing into my lungs, the thoughts slowing down. The panic drains away, and I sag in relief.

My head is clear now. I'll sell some art; I'll do whatever it takes to keep seeing Carolyn. She's the only thing standing between me and the black endlessness of despair. She's the only thing keeping me from using my knife for permanent relief.

I grab handfuls of tissues and press them hard against my arm until the bleeding stops. Then I sit back and look at the colored pencils and markers, the bottles of gouache, and the pastels scattered over my desk. There's something comforting about all that disorganized color just waiting to be used.

I pick up a pencil, rolling it between my fingers. It felt unbearable today, needing to cut so badly and not being able to; not having anything to cut with until I picked up the knife in class. But I'd rather have my own, the one I'm comfortable with. The one I've used so many times.

I wipe the blood off my utility knife with a tissue, then snap the top section of the blade off, starting a new edge so it'll be sharp for next time. The sharpness is important; it gives me more control. I press it against my skin, knowing I could plunge it right through my flesh, but knowing I won't, not right now.

I exhale. I can't go through another day like today. I *need* to have my knife with me. But if I carry it around, even stuffed in my bag, someone will notice. It's too bulky—and too bright, with the neon yellow plastic. I push the blade right up through the top of the plastic handle, un-hooking it from the knob that keeps it in place. It falls into my palm, thin and light. The blade is flat, no wider than my finger, and fits neatly in my hand. I tuck it into my back pocket, where it lies snug against my jeans.

"Kendra, honey, are you all right?" Mom asks, knocking on the door.

I slap on a sterile pad, half twist the greying gauze around my arm, and yank my sleeve down. Then I ram the empty handle of the utility knife beneath the covers and toss the broken tip into my garbage can.

"Kendra?" Mom rattles the doorknob.

I look around, trying to see what I've missed, what I don't want her to see. My hands shake. "Just a second!"

"Kendra, let me in. I know you're upset."

I stuff the bloody tissues into my garbage, crumpling clean ones on top. Then I drag the chair away and open the door.

Mom's standing there, like she doesn't know what to say. "Kendra . . . " Her voice wobbles. "Are you all right?"

I lick my lips. "I'm fine. I'm just—I'm upset, okay?"

She cranes her neck and looks around, her eyes scanning the room. Socks, sketchbooks, and comic books lie on the floor. My unmade bed, the usual mess on my desk— that's all there is to see. At least, I hope that's all.

"What were you doing in here?"

"Nothing!"

Mom keeps watching me, as if looking at me long enough will make the secret pop right out of my mouth.

"God! Can't I have any privacy around here?"

"I wish you'd talk to me."

"I did! I am." I cross my arms over my chest. "I'm not going to quit therapy. I'll get a job after school, do whatever I have to, but I'm not going to quit!"

"Honey, we're not trying to make life harder for you. You can keep seeing Carolyn. We'll manage somehow."

"How? How are you going to manage, if you can't afford it?"

"A few shops owe me money," Mom says. "You know how I am about keeping after them. Well, this time I'm going to be firm. We need that money. That'll hold us for a while. And after that, we'll see. I don't want you to worry, all right?"

Her voice is upbeat, but there's tension beneath it.

I wonder if she's thinking about the time she caught

me going through the medicine cabinet, stacking up the bottles of pills before they put me into therapy—before Protective Services ordered them to send me. Before Sandy called the police. Maybe Mom puts a positive spin on everything because she can't bear the way things are. Maybe that's her way of staying sane, like cutting is mine.

"Thanks, Mom," I say. "That means a lot." I almost feel like hugging her.

Mom smiles, bright as a toothpaste commercial. "And who knows? Maybe you won't need to see her for very long."

Her words are like a slap, bringing me back to reality. I step back and she follows me, her face practically in mine.

"Honey, it's okay. We'll find a way for you to see her as long as you need to."

Like I believe that.

I have to come up with the money myself. Sell my art—if anyone will buy it. Mom's paintings are picturesque views of the world, little postcards of happiness, while mine are all emotion and color. Mine tap into my pain and grief and sometimes into my happiness, but always into something that comes from deep inside. No boats in the harbor or sunlit meadows for me. I do my art because I have to. Paint or cut—they both help me survive. But Mom paints for the money—and her art sells. People want those perfect postcards of the world. I don't think they want messy emotion. But I have to try.

Tires crunch on our driveway. Dad's home.

Mom bites her lip. "Listen, Kendra, don't say anything to your father, all right? He's taking this downsizing thing very hard. He'll feel horrible if he knows you're upset."

So suck it up and smile. What else is new? "Okay."

It doesn't matter, anyway. It's not like he could change what's happening.

"Good girl." Mom starts down the hall. "Dinner's in half an hour."

The side door slams. "I'm home!" Dad calls.

I drag my portfolio out of my closet and start going through all my paintings. I dump the really painful ones in a box at my feet—the automatic reject pile. Anything that doesn't look well-crafted goes in there, too. But everything else stays out.

Footsteps thump down the hall. I ram the box into my closet and slap clothes on top. No one's ever seen my abuse art. No one except Carolyn and Sandy—and they've only seen a few.

Dad pokes his head through the doorway. "Knock, knock. Can I come in?"

"Sure."

He looks haggard, with dark, puffy shadows beneath his eyes, the deep lines around his mouth more pronounced than usual. There are huge sweat stains under his armpits of his crumpled shirt, and his tie is loose around his neck, like he only half pulled it off. I haven't seen him look like this since the night he found out about the abuse. Since the night Protective Services came to our house.

He rubs a hand across his face. "Did your mother tell you—"

"Yeah, she did," I say it fast, so he doesn't have to.

"It won't be forever, Kendra. Just until I can get back on my feet."

"I know. It's okay."

Dad motions to my bed. "May I?"

I push a stack of paintings back, clearing a space for him.

He sits down heavily, the bedsprings creaking. "So—how are things?"

"Fine." *What is this—Probe Kendra Day?*

"Fine." Dad raises one eyebrow. "Fine as in 'I'm doing pretty good' or fine as in 'I had a lousy day and why won't you leave me alone'?"

"Daa–ad," I say, but I have to laugh.

"No, I'm serious. Because your mom seems to think it was the latter."

Why does she do this to me? I shrug. "Things are okay enough."

Dad searches my face, like he's trying to see everything I'm not telling him. "You had therapy today, right? How did that go?"

A lot better before I knew I was going to have to cut back. "It was okay."

"Do you think she's helping you?"

I pull my knees up to my chest. *Something's going on. They can't have found out about the cutting; they'd be freaking out if they had. But something's up, more than just money being tight.* "Yes; can't you tell?"

"No, really, Kendra, I need to know. Because if you truly think she's helping you, then we'll just have to cut corners somewhere else. Maybe we can take out a loan."

My mouth tastes like metal. What a choice: make myself feel better or put my family into debt. I know what I have to do. "She helps me, a lot. But I can cut back for a while. It's no biggie."

Dad looks relieved. "Are you sure?"

"Absolutely," I say, keeping my voice firm. The painting in front of me shimmers.

Dad picks it up. I grow still. I wish I'd hidden all the paintings before he came in. The one he's looking at shows a girl flying close to the sun, laughing with the happiness of being able to fly, not seeming to notice that her flesh is melting off her body like wax.

"I haven't seen your art in a while," Dad says. "It's very good. You're one talented young lady."

I stop myself from rolling my eyes. If he says that one more time, I'm going to get it tattooed somewhere.

Dad taps the painting. "Is this how you feel?"

I glance at it casually, like I haven't been staring at it. "Sometimes."

Dad goes silent.

I grit my teeth.

"It hurts a lot, doesn't it?" Dad says quietly. "What that man did to you."

I nod, my lips quivering. I clench my hands; I won't let myself cry.

"I'm sorry," Dad says. He puts his hand on mine.

I jerk away reflexively. A hurt look crosses his face.

"I'm sorry," I say. "I just—"

"Overreacted," Dad says. "I understand. But you can't let what happened to you affect all your relationships with men." He stands up. "It isn't healthy."

That's what therapy is for. But I don't say that.

After supper, I grab my portfolio and head off to Sandy's. There's a note taped to his door: "Kendra—come right in." I can hear the steady thump of music right through his closed door, and beneath the rhythm, I can just make out the whir of his pottery wheel.

I walk through his kitchen to his workroom. Sandy's bobbing his head to the music, his hands covered in wet clay as he works at the wheel, his sleeves neatly rolled up past his elbows. I stop in the doorway and watch. It never fails to look like magic, the way Sandy can pull a vase or a bowl out of a blob of clay.

Sandy shuts off the wheel and cuts the vase off the base with a piece of wire.

"I wish I could do that!" I shout.

He looks up, happy to see me. He wipes his hands on his apron and turns off the stereo. "You wanna sit down and have a try?"

I shake my head. "Not today." And not any day in the near future. He'd know something was wrong if I didn't roll up my sleeves, and I can't do that without him seeing what

I've done. I miss the feeling of the cool, squishy clay beneath my fingers, the whir of the wheel—but my creations always collapse or turn out lopsided anyway. Pencils and paint are more my thing.

Sandy hangs his apron on the hook behind him. "The books are in the kitchen. Emil brought them over last night."

I follow him back into the bright, airy room. It's like a designer kitchen on a budget, with fake marble countertops, halogen lights, and used but top-quality appliances. Stainless steel pans and pots hang from hooks in the ceiling alongside dried herbs from his garden. Sandy takes his cooking almost as seriously as his pottery.

I head over to the yellowed pine table where a bunch of hardcover art books are fanned out in a half circle, a vase of pink rosebuds behind them. The roses fill the room with their scent.

I nudge him. "I see that's not all Emil brought you."

Sandy blushes right up to the roots of his ginger hair. "Emil's a sweetheart."

"And it doesn't hurt that he's cute!"

"Ah, Kendra, you know me too well," Sandy says, slapping his chest and smiling. He and Emil make a handsome couple—light and dark, muscular and thin, both of them with kind faces and gentle eyes. If they ever raise a child together, that kid will be so lucky, growing up in a house full of love.

I start flipping through the books. The vibrant colors and textures are like music, the artists' voices each singing in their own tone, yet coming together in a richness that stirs my creativity. The artwork feeds my soul, giving me something I need. But I can't take the books home, or Mom will know I'm still painting.

"Thank you! I love them."

"Kendra—"

Something in his voice makes me look up. He's got that worried frown between his eyes again.

"Your mother called."

"Again? Okay…"

"She asked me how I thought you were doing."

I let go of the book. "You didn't tell her—"

"No; it's none of her business what we talk about."

I let out my breath. "I'll bet she didn't like that."

"She didn't." He clears his throat. "She also told me your dad got downsized. I know how much you rely on Carolyn. I'd like to pay for your next few sessions."

I can't accept. Money's tight for Sandy. And how could I ever pay him back? Yet I want to accept his offer so badly. Heat flares in my cheeks.

"I can't let you do that."

"Sure you can. You know I'd pay for more, if I could afford it. Let me do this; it'll make me feel good. I wish I'd had a therapist when I was your age. It would have saved me a lot of grief."

I wrestle with myself. But I need therapy, and I know Sandy means it. "All right. Thank you." Crisis put off—at least for the next week or so. I set my portfolio down on the table. "But I still need a way to pay for the rest. I thought you might know where to sell these."

Sandy sits down beside me, unzipping my portfolio. He goes through the paintings one by one, sometimes quickly, sometimes slowly, but always silently. Now and then, he nods or picks one up to study it.

My mouth feels too dry to swallow. I've never shown anyone so much of my art before, especially not all at once. I've never let anyone see so much of me, revealed so much of myself. Because it's my self that I'm showing—I have no doubt about that—my hopes and dreams, my nightmares and memories, all mixed together with bits of my soul.

Maybe I should have left some of the paintings at home. Especially the one he just uncovered—a naked girl with thick white bandages half covering her crotch and screaming mouth. I hadn't even thought about the bandages, about what they might be saying. My heart pounds in my ears, but Sandy flips the painting over and looks at the next one—and the next.

I unclench my hands. Some of the paintings seem happy, until you look closer and see the corner of pain—the tree woman with an axe sticking out of the earth near her roots; the child holding a ball of light, a look of wonder on her face, while blood drips from her cracked hands. I don't know why I can't paint happy. Maybe I'm afraid I'll end up dead inside, like Mom. Or maybe I just know pain better than anything else.

Sandy picks up the next painting, and I catch my breath. I don't know how I could have let this one slip by—a girl climbing up the edge of a utility knife, her arms and legs gouged open to the bone. How much more obvious—

and stupid—could I be? My breath is high and tight in my chest. I clench my hands in my lap, willing Sandy to put the painting down and pick up the next one.

Sandy looks at me, his eyes dark and worried. "Is there anything I should know?"

"No," I squeak.

He keeps looking at me and I can't look away.

"Kendra, I know how much it hurts. Sometimes it can get so bad, you think you can't survive it. But you can. You will."

Oh, God. Don't let him know. I push back my chair, ready to run.

Sandy sets the painting down. "You're not thinking of killing yourself, are you?"

I'm so relieved I almost laugh. "Not right now."

"Good. Because you have so much to live for, Kendra. You're bright and talented—and things will get better for you, I promise." Sandy reaches over and takes my hand, holds it in both his huge ones, his face serious. "If anything ever happened to you, I'd be devastated."

"It's okay, Sandy. I'm not thinking about suicide right now, I promise." *Not since I started cutting.* "Six months ago, maybe—but not right now."

"You telling me the truth? I read that gay teenagers are three times more likely to kill themselves than straight ones—" He looks at me intently.

"Yes! I swear."

"Well, you make sure you talk to me if you need to— any time, day or night." He clears his throat. "You're special to me, Kendra; you're like the daughter I never had. I care very much about what happens to you."

A warm spot grows in my belly. "I—thanks, Sandy."

"You betcha." He hugs me hard, his rough cheek warm against my skin.

Shadows flutter inside me—but it *can't* be Sandy. I need it not to be.

Sandy lets me go. "You okay?"

I nod and casually lean back.

"Well." Sandy stacks my paintings together. "Are you sure you want to sell these? Your art is—"

"Too personal?"

"I was going to say *powerful*. Once you sell them, you'll never be able to get them back."

I swallow hard. "I know. But I've got to be able to keep working with Carolyn."

"All right. Let me give these to Emil. He'll get them hung in the Java Cup; the owner is one of us. And maybe he can get them in a few galleries, too. Sound good?"

"Perfect! Thank you, Sandy." I hug him quickly. No shadows this time.

"And Kendra—if you decide you want to keep any of these pieces, just give me a call. I'd have no qualms about pulling them off the walls."

I laugh. "I will."

The phone shrills loudly.

I roll my eyes. "I'll bet that's my jailer, calling to check on me. I'd better get back."

"You want me to walk you home?"

"Nah, I'm okay."

It's dark outside, darker than when I left the house, and a few of the streetlights are out. There's a haze in the air like a thin fog, blurring everything. A cat screeches like someone stepped on its tail. I walk quickly past the parked cars, the rows of shadowy houses; some are still and dark,while others show the blue glow of TVs flickering in their windows.

Behind me, something rustles.

The hair rises on the back of my neck. I walk faster.

Footsteps echo behind me.

I spin around. Even through the gloom, I can see a man in a dark trench coat about a block away, a hat pulled down over his forehead, his face hidden in shadow.

My heart flutters. I start running, and the footsteps follow me, slowing when I slow, speeding up when I do. I'm sobbing, breath caught in my throat, and still the footsteps come, and I'm barely ahead of them.

I burst into the house, slam the door shut, and lock it. And then I stand there, shaking, until Mom comes to see who it is.

At school, I look for Meghan again. There's something about her that draws me to her. Maybe it's the tough-girl act that I know covers her vulnerability, or maybe it's that I know nobody sees her for who she really is. Just like nobody sees me—nobody except Carolyn and Sandy. And Sarah; Sarah used to.

Meghan's the first person who's interested me since Sarah left; she's the first person who's made me think I might want to open myself up again. But I don't see her anywhere, not even near Danny's charred locker. What if her mother's giving her problems? Or what if she got freaked out by my note?

I go to class when the bell rings, but I can't focus on what the teacher's saying. Whenever I start to relax, I hear the footsteps again. I keep my backpack on me, never letting it out of my sight. I'm afraid *he* knows that the art therapy group starts today, afraid that's what set him off.

Artists show so much through their art—and not always consciously. We show things in our choices of color or the lack of it; in what we decide to paint; and even in our brush strokes—like the way my mom's are so controlled, while mine are so fluid. Art is like a printout of my soul, showing all the things I can't say. And if *he's* near me still, if he's watching me, he already knows that.

Teachers' voices move in and out of my awareness like a weak radio signal. Even in art class, it's hard for me to keep my attention on Mrs. Archer. But I hear enough to know that we're drawing in black, white, and shades of grey today. It's a challenge that would normally have me leaping up to get my supplies before everyone else, but today I hang back, picking up whatever's left over.

Back at my seat, I stare at the blank page. The greys and blacks of charcoal and graphite remind me of the shadows, of *him*—and I can't let myself go there.

I clench my pencil, unable to make a mark on the page. Mrs. Archer walks past me slowly. I know she's noticed I haven't even started, but she doesn't say anything. She always seems to know when to push me and when to leave me alone.

I sketch a few light lines, erase them, then start again. *Meghan. Think of Meghan.*

I keep my mind focused on her as I work, shutting out everything else.

I draw Meghan's face, grinning cockily at me. I draw her with attitude, the tendrils of her hair becoming whips, keeping other people away. And I draw myself, coiled in one of her tendrils, her hair flowing up to join with mine. I rough out the background, filling it with texture that overlaps and intertwines.

Someone leans over me.

I jump.

"I didn't mean to startle you," Mrs. Archer says, touching my shoulder. "Do you mind if I take a look?"

"Of course not!"

Mrs. Archer sits down beside me, studying my drawing. I lean back and try to see with unclouded eyes.

The pencil strokes that make up Meghan's and my hair are soft and winding, sharp only at the tips, but the background is harsh, almost chaotic in pattern. The contrast works well, but it's somehow disturbing.

I stare harder and suck in my breath. The figure of a man, like a shadow, hovers in the background, his claw-like hands reaching toward one of the girls—towards me.

I glance quickly at Mrs. Archer, but I can't tell if she's seen it or not.

"This is very powerful, Kendra," she says. "The emotion, the depth—it truly affects the viewer."

"I've heard that before," I say wryly.

Mrs. Archer looks at me quizzically. "It's a *good* thing, Kendra. You make the viewer feel something when they look at your work. We need art like that in this world."

I look into her warm eyes, eyes that take me in. I don't know how she knew I'd heard what she said as a criticism—heard my mother's voice echoing in hers—but somehow she did. And then she gave me the reassurance I needed, without my even having to ask for it.

Mrs. Archer tilts her head. "I noticed you were having some trouble getting started today. Is everything all right at home?"

"Everything's fine!" I say quickly, my voice too bright—like my mom's.

Mrs. Archer looks like she doesn't quite believe me, but she nods, then goes back to my drawing. "The contrast works beautifully here. I wonder what would happen, though, if you heightened the contrast even more? If you brought these two figures"—she points to Meghan and me—"clearly into the forefront, and let the others take more of a backseat."

I look at the drawing, my interest quickening. That's *exactly* what I should do. The people Meghan's keeping away—they're peripheral, so they should look that way. And the man—I don't want him to be there at all, but he is. At least he's in the shadows, with his face obscured. He'll stay darker than the other figures—he needs to be; it's who he is. But the two girls will stand out like they're filled with light.

"I get it!" I say. "Thank you."

Mrs. Archer laughs as she stands. "It's all you, Kendra."

I go back to my drawing, working feverishly now, wanting to get it finished before the period ends. As I add the layers, the figures advance or recede, the way I thought they would.

The bell rings, snapping me out of my concentration. I shove my sketchbook into my bag, take my materials back up to the front, then stand waiting for Mrs. Archer to finish with another student.

She turns to me.

"It worked perfectly," I say. "Thank you."

Mrs. Archer shakes her head. "I just built on your idea. You're the one who took it there." She sets her notebook down on her desk. "I don't think you know how extraordinary you are, Kendra. I have several gifted students this year, though you're by far the most talented. But the others— they'd improve by leaps and bounds if they learned how to listen to suggestions other than their own once in a while. But you—you listen to an idea, figure out how and if it fits into your vision, and then you run with it."

She pauses, looks at me seriously. "I don't know if you know what you're going to do with your life, Kendra, but I hope you'll always create art. You've got a powerful voice and a lot to say. And I think, if you keep at it, you'll go quite far."

Wow. I take a step back, blinking. It feels wonderful and frightening, all at once, to have someone believe in me that much. I wish I could hang onto her voice instead of always hearing my mom's.

Behind me, kids are whispering and talking. The period has already started. I shift my weight onto one foot, then the other.

"Goodness! I shouldn't have kept you talking so long!" Mrs. Archer says. She scribbles out a late pass and hands it to me. "My apologies to your teacher."

She turns around and claps her hands. "All right, class! Enough chatter."

The rest of the classes flash by, teachers' voices just background noise. When the last bell rings, I head over to the community center, the folded sheet of directions in my hand. I pass rooms 410, 411, 412, and stop outside 415. And that's when I see her, sitting in the hallway. An electric charge runs through me.

"Meghan," I say.

She turns around and looks up at me, a wide smile slicing through the boredom on her face. "Hey. What're you in for?"

"In for?" I sit down next to her, our legs almost touching.

"Yeah. The court ordered me here; it's either take art therapy or do some time, just for burning a lousy locker. Can you believe that?" She lights a cigarette and takes a drag. "You here because you wanna be?"

I shrug. "I like art."

"Good, 'cause you're gonna get a whole lot of it stuffed down your throat."

"Whatever they do, it can't be as bad as my mom."

"She into art museums and all that crap?" Meghan blows her smoke away from me.

I try not to cough. "She's an artist."

"Oh." Meghan jiggles her foot. "So you must be really talented and all, with your mom an artist and everything."

"My mom doesn't think so. She says my art is too raw—that no one will ever want to buy it."

"Do they have to?" Meghan says. "I mean, that's not the point, is it?"

"No, I guess not. Not unless you want to make a living from it, the way my mom does."

"Yeah? What's she paint?"

"Landscapes. Scenery. Pretty pictures of cows in meadows with buttercups."

Meghan snorts. "Like we need more lies telling us how perfect life is. I tell ya, what we need to see is the real stuff, stuff that shows what people usually hide. Maybe if somebody painted that, then we wouldn't all feel so alone."

Her voice drifts off, like she's not sure she should've said what she did.

I want to tell her that she can trust me, but that sounds like too much, too fast. So I just sit there, biting down on my lip, using the pain to keep myself quiet.

Meghan crushes the cigarette out on the bottom of her shoe, then pockets the stub.

Say something, idiot! But everything I can think of sounds stupid.

I look away from her and check out the hallway. It's like I never left school; the chairs lined up against the wall are an uncomfortable plastic orange like the ones in the cafeteria, and the speckled floor and cream-painted brick walls are just like the ones at school, impersonal and ugly. The building must've been designed by the same architect.

I glance at Meghan. I'm so aware of her shoulder almost touching mine, of the flowery smell of her shampoo, of how pretty she is. And how nervous. She's picking at the skin around her nails, the same way I do.

I touch her arm. "I like what you said."

"Yeah?"

"Yeah."

"Whew." Meghan nudges me with her shoulder. "Thought I'd struck something there."

I shake my head. "I just—I know that feeling. Like I'm alone, even though there're people all around me."

"Yeah," she says softly.

"Did you get my note?" I ask.

"You left me a note? What'd it say?" Meghan's eyebrows go up, her eyes bright.

"Uh—not much—I was just thanking you for standing up for me the other day."

Meghan laughs. "It was worth getting busted just to see that look on Danny's face. He deserved to get taken down." She touches my hand. "And it was worth it to help you. Definitely worth it."

We sit there, grinning at each other, and I feel that closeness again, that connection. I want to show her what I hide from others—want to show her my art. I unzip my backpack and feel around—and my hand closes on something small and hard. Something unfamiliar.

I pull it out of my bag, dreading what I'll see. It's a red flash MP3 player. And it's definitely not mine.

"What is it? What's wrong?"

I look closer. There's a printed label on the drive, but I can't get my eyes to focus. I blink, then blink again.

Meghan takes the MP3 player from me, rotating it in her fingers. "Nice. You don't have to worry if you lose it. You had it long?"

"No." My voice cracks.

Meghan hands it back to me. I stuff one ear-bud into my ear, press play. "You will learn to be silent," a deep, computer-generated voice intones.

I yank the ear-bud out, throw the player against the wall. The air is so stuffy and close I feel like I can't breathe.

"Hey." Meghan gets up, grabs the player. "Don't you want this any more?"

Weight presses down on me, heavy like his body, pushing out my breath. "You can have it," I choke out. I close my eyes. *It's from him—I'm sure of it.* I swallow down bile at the thought.

I hear the tinny, robotic voice faintly. I jerk my eyes open. Meghan's got the buds in her ears.

I tear the MP3 player out of her hands.

Meghan looks at me, her eyes all serious and worried. "Someone threatening you?"

"No. Just a joke," I say, trying to smile.

Meghan looks at me uncertainly. "Some joke."

I shrug.

She hands me the MP3 player, but I shove it back at her. "Keep it. Really."

"All right." Meghan drops it in her backpack, then hesitates, looking at me. "Seriously—is someone bothering you?"

"No!" I shake my head so hard I can almost feel my brain rocking around inside my skull. "I'm fine, okay?" I force the tears back.

"Okay," Meghan says, "I've forgotten it." Her voice is soft, almost hurt.

I want to tell her that she's not the one I don't trust; it's *him*. I'm scared he'll find out somehow. But the words stay lodged inside me like pebbles, cramping my stomach.

Meghan flips her hair over her shoulder, and I catch a glimpse of purple yellow brown, the colors so startling there on the back of her neck.

"Who did that to you?"

Meghan's gaze snaps to mine. "Nobody," she says, trying to cover the bruise. "It's nothing, all right? She doesn't always know what she's doing."

"Who doesn't?" But I already know: the booze-drinking mother. "I'm sorry."

"It's no big deal." Meghan's eyes are wary. "Don't say anything, okay? Promise you won't." She grabs my hand. "I know what it's like in foster homes. It can be a helluva lot worse than what I have now. I'm just waiting, saving up money till I can get out. So don't blow it for me, 'kay?"

I nod slowly. I'm not sure it's the right thing to do, but I think of how she let the MP3 slide, think of how I'd feel if she knew about *him*, and I nod again.

Meghan releases my hand, and I'm almost sorry she's let go. She rocks her chair back against the wall and sighs loudly. "God, when are they going to start this thing? It's worse than the first day of school."

Footsteps click-clack down the hall. I look up to see Mrs. Archer appear around the corner. "Hi, Kendra; hi, Meghan."

Mrs. Archer? I sit up straighter, my heart racing.

Meghan sets her chair down with a thud. "What are *you* doing here?"

"I'm training to be an art therapist," Mrs. Archer says, her smile faltering.

Meghan crosses her arms. "Oh, great. Now I have school *after* school, too."

"I didn't realize you'd both be here. If it makes either of you uncomfortable, I can talk to the instructor and get reassigned."

"It's okay with me," I say. "I'm just glad it's you and not Mr. Blair."

"Yeah," Meghan says. "Sorry, Mrs. A. It was just the shock—seeing a teacher and all."

Mrs. Archer laughs. "Not too big a shock, I hope." She looks around. "Where are the others?"

"The others?"

"There should be six of you."

"I've been waiting here since three, and there haven't been any others," Meghan says.

"That's strange." Mrs. Archer purses her lips.

I get this sinking feeling in my stomach. *What if we're in the wrong place or everybody's gone in already?* "Maybe there's another entrance?" Meghan and I look at each other. I know neither of us wants to walk in there—not with everybody staring.

But at least we won't be alone. There are three of us now: me, Meghan, and Mrs. Archer.

10

Everyone turns to look at us when we enter the art therapy room. Four kids our age and the therapist, all sitting around a long wooden table. One boy leans back, looking bored with us all, but I can see his leg moving like a jackhammer under the table. Another is short and stout, with more pimples than skin covering his sullen face. The girl closest to me is chewing her gum open-mouthed, the sound so loud it almost sounds like she's talking. The other girl's face is bowed so low that all I can see is the top of her head.

The only one who looks the least bit friendly is the therapist. She's a tall, thin woman with long grey-black hair, dressed in the clothes of a working-artist: a T-shirt, paint-stained jeans, and sandals. She beams at us, then says, "Ah, good. There you are. Welcome. I'm Julie." She motions toward Mrs. Archer. "And this is Eileen. She'll be joining us every week and helping me out as a part of her training. I hope you'll be nice to her. Now, if the two of you would take a seat, we'll begin."

I sit as far away from the others as I can, realizing even as I do it that it sets me apart, but I can't seem to stop myself. Already I'm stiffening up inside, preparing for the isolation I've created—but then Meghan plops down in the chair beside me and I relax.

I take a deep breath and look around. The walls are the same ugly cream in here. And the supplies are so meager. All we have are large pieces of manila paper spread out on the table, along with jugs of crayons and big, flat paintbrushes with rough synthetic bristles that come off while you paint. Bottles of cheap tempera and cans of water sit in the center. Next to them are chunks of Styrofoam and wood, empty spools, cardboard tubes, glue, and wire. It's like what you'd give to a bunch of kindergartners. I slump in my seat.

"I know some of you are artists," Julie says, "and I'm sorry we don't have anything better to use. My supplier went bankrupt and didn't bother to tell me. I should have some better materials for you by next week."

She looks around at all of us. "Some of you are probably nervous, wondering how this works. Let me tell you right now that no one's art will be judged here—not by me and not by anyone else. The goal isn't to create something artistically pleasing, but rather to express yourself. I don't want you to think about how it looks. Instead, I want you to paint what you feel."

I shift uneasily in my seat. She's telling us the opposite of everything I've learned about technique. How a painting looks is what communicates the feeling. And aren't we supposed to be expressing feelings?

Julie looks at me like she knows what I'm thinking, and I duck my head, avoiding her eyes.

"Any questions?" she asks.

"What are we supposed to draw?" the pimple-faced boy asks.

"Anything you like, Peter. It just has to come from inside you."

"Gee, maybe I'll draw my blood and guts," Meghan mutters.

Giggles bubble up inside me, frothy and chaotic. I press my hand against my lips, holding back my laughter.

"If you'd like more direction, then draw how you see yourself right at this moment," Julie says. "Eileen and I will be walking around the table to talk with each of you. Meanwhile, go ahead and get started."

I bite the inside of my cheek. I don't even know if I should be here. If he can get into my backpack without my seeing him, he can probably get hold of the art I do here. I'll just have to make sure I don't let stuff out in my artwork—make sure there's nothing to show him what's started coming back to me.

Meghan grabs one of the big brushes and starts spreading thick, dark streaks of blue over her paper. She doesn't seem to care what her strokes will show. I pull out a crayon and roll it between my fingers. The scent of crisp paper and colored wax tugs at some sadness locked inside me.

I touch the crayon to the soft yellow paper. The deep color of the wax is rich and full, and I wonder why people think crayons are only for children. I long to draw, to let the crayon bring out the texture of the paper beneath it.

No. I can't. I set the crayon firmly down.

Julie's walking slowly around the room, stopping to comment here, encourage there. When she reaches me, she stands there for a long moment. She leans her hand against the table. "Having trouble?" she asks softly.

"I'm just considering my options," I say, picking my crayon back up, and tapping it against my lips like I'm thinking.

"I'd prefer you not plan it out," Julie says. "For art therapy, it's better to come right from your gut. I know you have some training in art, so it must be hard for you to let go of that, but I'd like you to try."

My ears heat up. I don't have any trouble creating art with feeling! I'm *not* my mom. I grip the crayon, wanting to show her. If I'm careful, if I keep *him* out of it, what can it hurt?

I make a light mark against the paper, then another, giving in to the longing. A girl's face appears, her mouth sewn shut with zigzags of black thread. In one hand is the needle, and in the other is a stitch ripper, its point jagged and sharp.

Somewhere in the back of my mind, I'm aware that Julie's moved away, but I hardly care. I keep drawing, pulling out the story from the paper. Blood speckles the tip of the stitch ripper, and one thread hangs loose from the girl's mouth.

I sketch in stormy skies behind the girl, and trees bending in the wind—though if I was following technique, I should have drawn those in first. I press the crayon so hard against the paper, it snaps. I can hear my mom, chiding me to be more careful. I draw even faster; and at the corner of the page, almost entirely out of the drawing, a man's hand appears, reaching for the girl.

"God, if you can do that with crayons, you must be dynamite with paint," Meghan says, leaning over my arm to look.

I come back to the room with a start. "It's just a sketch," I say, but she leans in closer. The gum-chewing girl gets up and comes over, too. I sink down in my chair. *So much for holding myself back.*

"Meghan, Stacey, please focus on your own work," Julie says. She walks over and looks at Meghan's page, then sits next to her. "This girl looks like she's been through something pretty awful," she says, smoothing out the paper. "Want to tell me about her?"

"Nope. It's just a fucking picture."

"I think it's more than that. I think it's trying to tell me something."

I sneak a glance. Meghan has crudely painted a girl with a smile stamped on her face, a brownish-yellow tattoo on her shoulder, and a beer bottle in her hand. *Brownish-yellow—like a bruise.* I glance at Meghan, sitting there so rigidly, and I know Julie's right. I want to say, "I'm sorry you're hurting," but I know that would only make it worse.

My stomach cramps. A shadow rises up inside me, smothering my breath. *His hand clutching my thigh. Yellow-brown marks beneath, like fingerprints, on my skin. A warm, sticky trail of blood and semen on my legs. His voice hissing, "I will kill you if you tell."*

I grip the edge of the table—and my drawing comes back into focus, the man's hand jumping out at me. *His* hand. There's something familiar about the blunt fingernails, the hair on his fingers, the way he holds his hand.

I can't draw air into my lungs. I look away, ignoring the spinning in my head, the sickness in my stomach. I don't know whose hand it is. I *don't!*

I hitch in a breath, then another.

"I tell you, it's just a picture," Meghan is saying. "Lay off with your analytical shit."

"Nothing is *just* a picture. Each one tells us something."

I hunch over my page, trying to block their view.

"The girl's fine," Meghan insists. "She's smiling."

"Sure, she's smiling," Julie says. "But it looks like she's trying to hide how she feels."

Meghan throws her brush down. "What is it with you people? You're not happy unless you dig something up, are you? Well, guess what? There's nothing for you to find!"

I try to shut out what she's saying. But the room is too small, her voice too harsh, and I'm drowning in the pain that fills the room.

"Nobody's hurt me!" Meghan shouts. "Nobody's snuck into my room at night and climbed into my bed, nobody's put an iron to my face. All right? I'm not some abused kid!"

Dark spots dance in front of me. *I'm rocking on a bed, pain like a knife between my legs and blood on the sheets. "If you tell, you will die," he says, his voice low and hoarse.* I can hear his voice now, can hear it as clearly as if he's right here beside me. But I can't let myself recognize his voice. I won't.

Images rip through my brain, pounding behind my eyes. *His huge body on top of mine, driving into me. My hands gripping the sheets. My body arched with pain.*

I shudder.

Meghan crumples up her painting and tosses it on the floor.

Julie reaches down and picks it up, smoothing it out.

"Just forget it!" Meghan yells, her voice breaking—breaking, the way I am inside. I feel the pain in her, as strong as my own. I feel her terror at being cornered, at someone trying to rip out the secrets embedded in her skin.

"Leave her alone!" I scream, leaping from my chair. "Just leave her alone!"

"I wasn't talking to you," Julie says. "I was talking to Meghan."

"But she doesn't *want* to talk!" I say, trembling. "Stop trying to make her!"

Everyone is staring at me, even Mrs. Archer. Especially Mrs. Archer. I sink back into my chair, my face burning. I've really done it now.

Julie rubs her hand over her eyes. "Maybe I did push a little too hard," she says, turning to Meghan. "I'm sorry."

"Hey, it's no skin off my back," Meghan says, but she looks close to tears. She pushes her hair out of her eyes and smiles, her lips quivering.

I can't smile back. I clench my hands under the table, digging my nails into my skin. I need to cut.

"Kendra? How're you doing?" Julie asks, resting a hand on my shoulder.

"Fine," I say. "Just fine."

11

Julie and Mrs. Archer look at each other across the table, and I know they don't believe me. I'm shaking so hard I can hear my teeth chatter.

Julie's hand is still on my shoulder. She leans down close. "Come outside with me."

I follow her out of the room, into the hallway. The fluorescent lights flicker and buzz.

Julie closes the door and looks at me, her eyes sad. "Something really upset you in there, didn't it?"

"I'm sorry. It won't happen again."

"That's not what worries me." Julie tilts her head to one side. "Why were you so upset when I was trying to get Meghan to talk?"

"Because sometimes it isn't safe to," I say without thinking. I close my mouth fast. I need to shut myself down right now. I need to cut.

"Sometimes it's not safe to," Julie says. "Is that what it's like for you?"

His hand, gripping my wrist. His lips against my ear.

I blink hard, pushing the shadows away. *I've got to think my way out of this. I've got to keep her from the truth.*

"I've got a therapist," I say. "Carolyn Fairchild. You can call her if you like. But I'm already dealing with it."

"I will kill you if you tell."

"I'm glad to hear that," Julie says.

I want to cut so bad, it's hard to concentrate. "I don't mean to be rude, but I have to go to the bathroom."

Julie studies me. "You're sure you don't want to—"

"I've really got to go."

"All right. But come straight back."

I force myself to walk slowly away—but as soon as I round the corner, out of her sight, I'm running, flying toward my release. I smash into the bathroom and shut myself into a stall.

I have the warm blade out of my pocket and into my hand almost before I have the door locked. I tear off the bandage and slash until I can't hear his voice any more, until I can't see his hands. I slash until the fear leaves me.

Then I clean up the blood and wrap my arm tightly, pulling my sleeve back down over my tender arm. When I walk back in, the whole room looks different—bigger, brighter, not so full of pain. I settle in next to Meghan and turn my paper over.

My head is clear again. The shadows are gone. I pick up the crayons and draw another picture, one that I know won't show too much—and the drawing spills out of me like I was meant to draw it. It shows two girls holding hands, smiling up at the clear blue sky. All around their bare feet are shards of glass, but the girls are safe where they stand.

Meghan reaches out beneath the table and rests her hand on my thigh. Her hand is warm and heavy, and I feel myself come back into my body, to the dull, throbbing pain in my arm, to the feeling of her hand on my jeans. Her hand feels good. Safe. Even comforting. I don't want her to move it away.

"You all right?" she whispers.

I nod. I can't tell her, but I'm better than I was before. I know how to stop the shadows now; how to keep them from coming into my art. I know how to keep myself safe. All I have to do is cut. Cut until it all bleeds away.

12

Julie stands, then says, "Sometimes art therapy can bring up a lot of emotion, so I'd like you all to be gentle with yourselves over the coming week. This was a good session, people; you should be proud of yourselves. I'll see you all again next Thursday; I know you'll be looking forward to it."

"She's a regular comedian, that one," Meghan mutters.

I laugh. I can *laugh* again.

Meghan and I roll up our art, fastening elastic bands around the sheets. We walk out of the room together, carrying the rolls of paper like sabers.

"You really saved my ass back there," Meghan says. "Thank you."

"I'm sorry I made such a scene."

"You kidding?" Meghan grins. "You took the heat right off *me!*" Her face grows serious. "You've been through some rough shit, haven't you?"

"Yeah. Kinda."

"You mind my asking what?"

I take a deep breath. With anyone else, I wouldn't go

there, but I trust Meghan. I like her. "Sexual abuse. When I was a kid. Started when I was two, maybe younger. I don't know when it stopped. I don't even remember who did it. Guess I don't want to."

Meghan whistles. "That's rough. Must be really hard sometimes, huh?"

"Yeah." My arm aches fiercely.

We walk quietly for a few minutes, our feet moving in rhythm.

Meghan glances at me. "Nobody gets what it's like. Not unless they've been there." "Sometimes I think it's screwed my whole life up, you know? I mean, I don't know what I would've been like if my mom never beat on me, but I think I'd probably be different. Not so messed up."

"Me, too!" I can't believe how much she understands. How alike we are.

We reach the exit. I wish we didn't have to say good-bye, but I don't want to push myself on her.

"Hey, you feel like getting something to eat?" Meghan asks.

I shove open the door, feel the sun on my face, smile so wide my mouth hurts. "Yeah! And I know just the place."

The Java Cup. I think it's a great idea until we get there—and then I start to curl up inside myself, retreating from my own skin. But I push open the door anyway and lead the way in. The delicious scents of chocolate and coffee wrap around me, and the haunting sound of pan flutes floats above the murmur of conversation, the sound so clear it's almost as if the musicians are in here with us.

I see my paintings almost before I see anything else;

they've been matted and framed and have little white cards on the walls beneath them. They look so professional. I raise my head. *That's my art on the walls! My art that people are looking at.* Sandy is *so* my fairy godfather.

"Hey, will you look at that art!" Meghan says. "It's something else."

My stomach jumps. "Do you like it?"

"Hell, yeah. It's real art—not that fake scenery or that squares and triangles stuff." Meghan scratches her cheek. "It kinda reminds me of your art."

I hold back my laughter. "That's because it is."

Meghan looks at me, eyes wide, her lips parted. She's so beautiful. "Get out!"

She walks up close to a painting and looks at my signature, then at the card beneath it. A giggle bursts out of me.

She whirls around and bops me on the head with her rolled-up painting. "You twit!" she says. "You little twit!" She bops me on the head again. I shield my head and laugh.

Meghan grabs my shoulders and turns me to face the tables of talking, laughing people. "Hey, everybody," Meghan says loudly. "This is my friend Kendra Marshall, the artist of these paintings!"

I clap my hand over her mouth, but most people are smiling at us—even the woman behind the counter.

"Stop that!" I hiss at Meghan, but I can feel a smile sneaking onto my face. I lead her by the hand to an empty table and push her into a chair as the woman from behind the counter comes over.

"Hi, Kendra, I'm Lisa. Emil told me all about you. I've

got something for you." Lisa takes a wad of bills out of her apron and pulls off five twenties. "One of your paintings sold. People really like them, but I told them they can't take them till you bring me more. So bring in some new ones real soon, you hear?"

"You got it." I take the money and stuff it into my pocket. Two sessions paid for, just like that!

Lisa takes our order. After she leaves, Meghan turns to me. "I don't care what your mom says; she's wrong. Your art is good, Kendra, real good. Not everything has to be pretty."

"I guess it doesn't," I say.

Happiness warms me through like the summer sun.

13

Mom's waiting at the screen door when I get home.

I sigh and walk toward her. "It went fine," I say, before she can ask me anything. I head to the kitchen and pour myself a glass of orange juice.

Mom hovers around me. "Why is it that you can't paint with me, but you can with a bunch of strangers?"

Because they don't criticize me. "I didn't paint. I drew. And it was different; it was about healing, not technique."

"Can I at least see what you did?"

I stare at the bright yellow walls of the kitchen until my eyes ache. "I don't think it's the kind of art you like."

"I've never said I didn't like your art, Kendra."

"Yes, you did!"

"I've said that some of your art won't sell, that it's not what people want to look at."

"Isn't that the same thing?"

Mom winces. "I've always encouraged you! Didn't I buy you your first set of paints? Didn't I give you all the art supplies you ever wanted?" Her lips tighten. "You have talent, Kendra. A lot of talent. I just hate to see you waste it."

I lean back against the fridge, cross my arms over my chest. "It's not wasting it if it helps me. Isn't that what art is supposed to be about? Expression?"

"Art is about many things. But it won't mean much if you don't hone your talent. Now, are you going to let me see what you did, or not?"

If I say no, she'll hound me until I say yes. I sigh and pull the drawing out of my backpack.

Mom plucks it from me and unrolls it. She frowns at the girl with her mouth sewn shut.

"Aren't you going to say anything?" I ask.

"It's . . . good," Mom says, almost like it hurts her to say it.

I grit my teeth. "All right, what's wrong with it?"

"No one's ever going to want to look at this, let alone buy it. It's depressing."

I snatch the drawing back, stuff it into my bag. "I knew you couldn't look at my art without criticizing it!"

"You asked me! I'm only trying to help prepare you for the real world. It's harsh out there—"

"Do you think I don't know that? The first time that man raped me, I knew that—"

"So why do you want to make things harder for yourself? How are you ever going to survive if you can't sell your art?"

"Who says I can't?" The words bounce off the walls. I wish I could swallow them back.

"You sold your art? Why didn't you tell me? Who bought it? For how much?"

I can't tell if she's excited or angry. "Sandy helped me.

It was just a one-time thing." *I don't know why I'm lying to her. Yes, I do. I'm trying to protect myself. Trying to keep her from taking over.*

"Sandy? Why didn't you come to me?"

Because I didn't think you'd help me. "I got a hundred dollars, Mom! And I don't know who bought it. I didn't ask."

She turns away from me, picks up a dishrag and scrubs at the counter. Her shoulders hunch, and her head bows.

"Mom?"

She doesn't turn around.

My stomach tightens. "Mom? What is it?"

"I'm happy for you," she says thickly.

I push off the fridge, go over and touch her back. She stiffens. Her face is all scrunched up, her nose red, her chin trembling; it's just the way my face gets when I'm trying not to cry. "Mom, what's wrong?"

She sniffs. "I thought *I* was going to be the one to introduce you to the art world. I thought we'd be so close. When you picked up your first crayon and imitated me, I knew we would be. But we've never been that way. Ever since you were a toddler, you've pulled away from me. And nothing I ever did could change that."

A memory rises up inside me, sharp and bitter. *I'm three, maybe four. We've just come back from a long day of visiting my parents' friends. I'm whimpering, holding my crotch, telling Mom's back that it hurts.*

Mom turns around from her painting, looking irritated. "What's wrong now?"

I keep whimpering.

"Kendra, I don't have time for this. Ask Daddy to fix it." And she turns away from me.

I snatch my hand from her back. Her shoulders are still hunched, the dishrag clenched in her hand. I can't believe she ignored me when I tried to tell her. Can't believe she didn't see my pain. Anger sits like a smouldering piece of coal in my stomach.

"Mom, do you remember when I tried to tell you—"

"You just shut me and your dad right out. I was worried about you! I told the family doctor, but he said it was normal, that you were learning to be independent. I never should have listened to him."

"Do you remember—"

"Your dad was always the better parent, making time for you, hugging your hurts away when I never could. I envied your relationship, the ease between you two—but believe me, Kendra, I'm a better parent than my parents ever were. They never touched me, except to hit me. I told you that, didn't I?"

She never talks to me like this. Never. It's almost like she knows what I've remembered and doesn't want to hear it.

"Mom—will you just *listen* to me?"

"I *am* listening." She scrubs the counter roughly, as if it's covered in stains.

"I tried to tell you about the abuse once, when I was three or four. Do you remember?"

Mom goes still. "Yes," she says. "I've thought about that every day since you told us—every single day! If only I'd listened to you then, things would be different. I blame myself, Kendra. I really do."

This isn't how I expected her to respond. I don't know what to say. I want to tell her that it's all right—but it's not. And it won't ever be.

"We didn't know as much back then," Mom says quickly. "We didn't know about child abuse, the way mothers seem to now. If I'd thought—if I'd understood—"

Another excuse. You can see when someone's been hurt like I was. It's obvious. Something changes in their eyes; pain becomes their center, even when they try to hide it. Like Meghan's eyes; I know my eyes have it, too. There's no way to miss it; it almost hurts to see.

I told them in so many ways: jumping at everyone's touch, keeping quiet to avoid too much attention, and hiding my body in loose clothes. Even my art screamed for help. I don't believe she didn't see it. Didn't *want* to see it—now that, I believe.

The clock over the stove ticks loudly, counting every second of our silence. The night sky is so black outside the kitchen window, it seems to absorb everything, even the stars.

Mom sets the dishrag down and looks at me, her eyes full of tears. I know she's asking for forgiveness, for understanding. But I have none to give her.

"I have to get my homework done." I turn away.

14

"Kendra—wait!"

I sigh and turn around. "What?"

"I'm sorry."

I nod. That's all I can do.

"Kendra—I know this isn't a good time, but I need to talk to you before your dad gets home."

Now what?

"I don't think there's an easy way to say this, so I'll just say it. It looks like we're going to have to move."

"What? Where?" I stare at her.

"Out of the city. Now that your dad's income's been cut in half, we're looking to lower our expenses. It would mean you couldn't see Carolyn any more or go to your art therapy—"

My breath is gone, punched out by her words. I sag against the wall, staring at the row of vitamin bottles that Mom's alphabetized. "I thought we already talked about this! I thought I could keep going."

"I know, honey. I'm sorry. I don't want to move,

either. We've been here twenty-six years and I love this place. But we may not have a choice."

I can't grasp what she's saying. "I told you, I'll pay for therapy. I'll get a part-time job, help out around here more—"

"Honey, that's not it. It's the loans, the bills—it's things that we can't control."

"Can't you get another loan? Talk to the bank?"

Mom purses her lips. "Your father tried just this morning. They turned him down."

My hands are fists. I want to smash something. "Why can't we just move to a smaller house? An apartment, even? Why do we have to move so far away?"

Mom picks up a bottle of hand cream, then sets it back down. "Houses are significantly cheaper in the suburbs, Kendra. And your dad and I—we've been worried about you for a while, now. You're retreating further from us, becoming even more withdrawn and moody. I guess we thought the change might do you some good."

I can feel the blood rising in my face, the tears starting in my eyes. "How do you think yanking me out of therapy will help? Or out of school or away from my friends? I need them! I need—"

I want to smash my hand through the window, let the glass rip into my skin. I want to make the pain go away.

"Yes? What do you need?"

"I need Carolyn, Mom. I can't face it all alone!" *His hand, gripping my wrist. His breath against my cheek.*

"You're not alone, honey," Mom says. "You've got us."

A scream rises inside me. "Don't you get it? You're

not enough!" The words are out before I can stop them. Hard, hurtful words. But the truth.

Mom turns her face away and I can see she's trying not to cry.

I dig my hand into my pocket, close my fingers around the blade, and let the edge bite into me, press against my flesh. "I'm sorry," I say. "I'm sorry. It's just—you're not a therapist, Mom. I need someone who knows what she's doing. I need someone who understands."

Mom's face twists in anger. "I've read every book on sexual abuse I could find! I've joined a support group. I've done everything I'm supposed to! Why aren't I ever enough for you?"

Oh God, she's melting down, and I don't know how to fix it. "Mom—"

"Don't you *Mom* me! I've worked damn hard at trying to be there for you, at trying to make things up to you. But you never let me in!"

I think of showing her my arm, of sharing *that* with her—but I'm not that stupid.

"You never told me," I say. "How do you expect me to know you've read about it when you hide the books like they're something shameful, some dirty secret?"

"That's not fair!" Mom cries. "I didn't want to burden you."

"But you weren't letting me in, either," I say. "And—" I try to shove down the words, but they're spewing out of me like vomit— "I don't feel like I can talk to you. You're always turning everything around, twisting what I say into a positive—or into a criticism of you."

I wrap my arms around myself and hold on tight. "If you really want me to talk to you, then I need you to hear what I have to say; you have to *listen*. If you're willing to do that, then I'm willing to try. But that won't change how much I need Carolyn."

Mom's lips tighten so much that they turn white.

I rush on. "I need someone who knows about abuse and knows how to help me deal with it. I need someone who's not family. And that someone is Carolyn."

"I'll bet you wish she was me, don't you, Kendra? I'll bet you wish she was your mother. I can see it in your eyes; I can hear it in the way you talk about her."

I don't say anything. *It's true.*

Mom puts her hands on her hips. "Well, I've got news for you, Kendra. Your Carolyn isn't as great as you think. Your Carolyn, your precious Carolyn, only understands so much because she was raped, too. She's a sexual abuse survivor."

My head feels like it's squeezing inward. *I can't take any more.*

Mom nods, a thin smile on her lips. "Yes, that's why she's *so* understanding. She's a victim herself. You think I should go get raped, just so I can understand you?"

"You don't understand anything!" I yell. And then I'm running out of the house and into the night, Mom screaming after me.

15

I run fast and hard, my shoes pounding against the pavement, jarring my bones. *Carolyn, a sexual abuse survivor.* It all fits now: the empathic looks, the sadness in her eyes I sometimes catch, the way she really gets my fear and pain. The way she understands me.

Why did she hide it from me? Why didn't she trust me enough to tell me?

My blade is in my pocket. I can't stop thinking about how much I want to cut, how much I need that comfort. All I'd have to do is duck into the bathroom of some all-night coffee shop....

I reach for my blade, and my fingers touch the smooth warmth of the stone instead. I take it out and press it against my cheek, remembering the tenderness in Carolyn's eyes as she offered me the basket of shells and stones.

Carolyn is still Carolyn. Even if she didn't tell me herself, it doesn't change the way she's been there for me. Or how much she cares.

I slow down.

Or maybe it does change things. She understands on a

gut level what I'm talking about—and she's made it to the other side. She's happy, and she's got a life that doesn't revolve around pain. I want that so bad—but I never believed I could have it. But if Carolyn can do it, maybe I can, too. I just have to hold onto what makes me happy. Carolyn. Meghan. Sandy. Mrs. Archer. And my art.

My cell rings. Mom. I can't talk to her right now, not without screaming. I shut my cell off and keep running, not even knowing where I'm going, until I find myself in front of Sandy's. His kitchen windows are warm squares of yellow light pushing back the darkness.

I raise my hand to knock.

Sandy swings open the door before I do, letting light and the warm aroma of garlic and tomato out into the night. "Kendra! I'm glad you're okay," he says. "Come on in." He opens the door wider.

Why wouldn't I be okay?

Sandy shuts the door on the night, then ushers me into the kitchen. The table is laid out with dishes: a bowl of asparagus and slivered almonds; a plate of crusty bread; bowls of pasta with cherry tomatoes, mushrooms, and some kind of herb on top. There are two half-drunk glasses of wine.

Emil stands, wiping at his mouth with a cloth napkin. He picks up the bottle of wine. "Good to see you, Kendra," he says, coming around the table and hugging me with one arm. "I'll just be in the living room, if either of you need me."

He kisses Sandy, and leaves.

I look at their half-eaten meal. *I shouldn't be here.* I turn to Sandy. "I should have called first. I'm sorry!"

"Nonsense," Sandy says firmly, steering me to the

table and sitting me down. "You are welcome here any time, day or night. You know that." He ruffles my hair, takes a plate down from the cupboard. "Have you eaten? Would you like some pasta? It's good, if I say so myself."

I bow my head. "No, thanks."

Sandy sits down across from me. "I'm glad you came to me. I was worried."

"My mother called you," I say slowly.

"When you ran off like that, she was scared. We all hoped you'd come here."

I hate that my mom can interfere in my friendship with Sandy like that. That she can call him and tell him her side of things before I even get a chance to. I cross my arms over my chest.

"So, you want to tell me what's going on?" Sandy asks, leaning forward.

"Why? Didn't she already tell you everything?" I slouch down in my chair.

"Kendra." Sandy reaches for my hand. "Your mom told me a few things, it's true. But that's between her and me as friends. I try to keep that separate—as separate as I can. I want to hear what's going on with *you*. I can see you're upset."

"They're talking about moving, Sandy—right out of the city!" I say. "I need my therapy! God, I don't know how I would have gotten through the last few months without it. Or without you. It's like ripping my life supports away." I swallow. "And things were just starting to get better. I met a girl I like—"

Sandy's eyes light up.

"I don't know where that's going," I say quickly. "I need time to find out. But most of all—I need to stay around the people who love me. Carolyn, and *you*. It's too hard alone."

"I know you need us," Sandy says. "If you have to move, I promise we'll stay in touch. You're important to me, Kendra. No way am I letting you out of my life that easily." He squeezes my hand. "Your parents love you, too, though."

I choke back the tears. I realize now that I was hoping Sandy would let me stay with him. But Sandy's in an uncomfortable position, being friends with both my mom and me. Like being pulled apart by two opposing magnets. Still, I have to try.

I draw my hand away, pick at my cuticle. Try to keep the tears from coming. What do I do if he says no?

"Kendra?" Sandy says.

"Can I stay with you if my parents move?" I say it all in a rush, not looking at him. "I can't handle leaving here—" My voice wobbles. I clench my teeth, hating how weak I sound.

There's a silence. I look up and see Sandy's face shadowed with pain. "I want to help you; you know I do. But Kendra—you're a minor," he says, spreading his hands apart. "I don't have any legal right to keep you here. I'm not your guardian. If your parents want to stop you from staying here, they can do it." Sandy pushes his plate away. "But I promise you, I'll negotiate on your behalf. I'll try to get your mother to agree to let you stay here. It's craziness to take you away from your support system right now."

But my mother is bullheaded and close-minded, espe-

cially when it comes to me. She's always resented how close I am to Sandy—and to my dad, too. And I know Sandy feels he owes her, because she's the one who introduced him to the local art world.

"I shouldn't have asked you," I say, clenching my hands together.

"No, I'm glad you did," Sandy says. "I want you to be able to ask me for what you need. I might not always be able to give it, but if I can, I will."

Sandy takes a mouthful of wine, and swallows it. "I'll try to convince your mom that it's not in your best interest to move right now, and I'll let her know that I'd be happy to open my home to you. But you know how your mom gets about me being gay. She probably won't be able to stomach the idea of you staying under the same roof with me. She'll think I'm corrupting you." The pain in his face deepens.

"Why are you even friends with her, when you know she thinks like that?" I ask.

"Your mom's a good person," Sandy says. "And—"

"You owe her," I say.

"Well, yes, I do. Your mom helped connect me with the right people. I couldn't have established myself here so quickly if she hadn't. But that's not what I was going to say. Your mom tries to do the right thing, even when she doesn't know what it is. She just needs a little time—"

"A little? You guys have been friends for more than twenty years, and she's still homophobic!"

"She's changed a lot, Kendra. You wouldn't know it, but she has. But we're getting off track here."

"I didn't know we were on a track."

Sandy sits there silently. I look up at him.

"Kendra—the years I spent on the street were some of the worst years of my life. Worse even than all the homophobic crap I grew up with. Sometimes I don't know how I survived it." He reaches for my hand again. "I wouldn't ever want you to make the same mistake I did. Promise me that no matter how bad things seem, you'll always come to me before you try anything stupid." He squeezes my hand.

For a second, I wonder if Sandy's hand is *his* hand. But it can't be.

Tears well up in my eyes, and I look away. What's the point of turning to Sandy if he can't help me?

"We'll work something out, Kendra," he says. "I'll never leave you hanging. Now promise me you'll come to me—"

"I promise," I say.

Sandy's on my side. I know he is. But he'll try to convince my mom without breaking their friendship. And I'm not sure I have the right to ask him to do more.

Sandy's still looking at me worriedly.

"I'm not going to run away," I say. *At least, I don't think I am.* "And I promise I'll come to you if I get to that point."

"*Before* you get to that point," Sandy says determinedly.

"Right!"

The phone shrills from the other room. I stiffen. I just know it's my mom.

Sandy looks at me unhappily. The phone rings again. I hear Emil pick it up in the other room, hear his voice rumble.

"Sandy, it's Lori Marshall!" Emil calls.

"I have to tell her you're here," Sandy says quietly. "But I promise I won't tell her anything you said. I can probably convince her to let you stay the night...."

"No, that's okay."

"Sandy!" Emil shouts again.

"You sure?" Sandy asks, standing. "We'd be happy to have you."

"I'm sure."

Sandy shrugs, then goes to the living room.

I listen to his voice rise and fall, and I know she's giving him the third degree, probably for not calling her as soon as I got here.

I glare down at the table. She's probably not calling because she's worried about me. She's probably calling to make sure I'll be home before Dad is. Because *he'd* worry. "Don't worry your father"—I've heard that so many times. It's like she thinks he needs protecting—more than me.

He *was* devastated when he found out I'd been abused. He looked like the pain was going to rip him apart. But it was *me* that it happened to, damn it. I'm the one who was raped—over and over and over again.

I press my fingers against my lips. I can't think about *him* right now. Can't think about any of it. I have to figure out how to keep seeing Carolyn. How to stay here. And Sandy isn't it.

I push back my chair and stand.

Sandy strides back in, then stops when he sees me. "You leaving already? I told your mom you'd be here for at least another half hour or so—"

Good. "Don't tell her I've left, Sandy, okay? I need some time to think."

Sandy puts his hands on my shoulders, gazes down into my eyes. "You're not going to do anything stupid?"

"I'm not."

Sandy kisses my cheek. "Then go have your half hour or so of freedom. But make sure you call me when you get home, all right? I don't want to be sitting up worrying about you."

"I will."

Out on the street, I flip open my cell. If anyone can help me, it's Meghan. I call 411. There's a lot of Ellises in the directory, but only a few are listed under a woman's name. I accept the first one.

"Yeah? Whaddya want?" a woman's irritated voice asks.

"Is Meghan there?"

"I dunno. Let me check." The receiver clunks down. "Meghan? Meghan, get your ass down here!" The woman coughs, then picks up the phone again. "She'll be right down. Mind you don't stay on too long. I got an important call coming through."

"Yes, ma'am." Guess they don't have call waiting— if it's even the right number.

I keep walking, clutching my phone, trying to look confident in the dark—and unapproachable.

"Yeah?"

It's Meghan.

I grip the phone tighter. "Hi, Meghan? It's Kendra. Listen, do you know any place I can crash if I need to?"

"Why? What's wrong?"

"My parents. They're talking about moving out of the city. But I can't leave my therapist and the group—" *And you.* "I thought maybe if I can find some place to stay, they won't drag me with them."

"Well, you can crash with me if you're desperate. My mom would never know the difference."

I breathe out. "Thanks, Meghan." I snap my cell shut.

I'm not going to stop seeing Carolyn, even if I have to run away to keep on seeing her.

I start back towards home, and suddenly there are footsteps behind me—heavy and deliberate.

I spin around, but no one's there—just a torn chip bag fluttering along the sidewalk. I pound ahead, moving faster now, trying to pretend I'm not afraid, my heels slamming against the cement. My heart's pumping so hard, I think I'm going to choke.

I flip open my cell again, keep my finger on the speed dial key for Carolyn.

I hear the footsteps again—louder this time. I whirl around, peering into the darkness, the streetlights barely making a dent in the night. The cars and newspaper stands cast long shadows along the dirty sidewalk, shadows that a man could hide in. Broken glass glitters beneath a parking meter.

A muffled cough explodes into the quiet.

I jerk my head toward the sound. I don't see anything at first. Then I spot a shiny black shoe sticking out from behind a parked car. My heart jolts like it's been shocked with a defibrillator; I turn and run as fast as I can toward home.

A car passes me, driving slowly. I dodge away from it. My breath rasps in my ears.

The porch light glows like a beacon. I run toward it, gulping air. I can almost feel him behind me, reaching for me. I race up the stairs, leap onto the porch. There's movement in front of me, a shadow rising to block my way.

"No!" I cry.

The shadow moves into the light, and I see it's just Mom. She grabs me by the arms.

I hiss with pain.

"Don't ever do that to me again!" Mom says, shaking me.

"I'm sorry!"

"It's dangerous for a girl out alone at night. For any woman."

I know! I keep the words locked inside; I don't want to scare her. Yet a tiny part of me wants to scream that it was a lot more dangerous for me to be with one of her friends— or with a teacher or an uncle or someone she knew—than to be out alone in the dark, chased by some faceless stranger.

Her fingers dig angrily into my arm, making my wounds burn—but I'm angry, too. I lift my head high. "I'm not moving."

"You may not have a choice."

You're wrong. "Is Dad in yet?"

"He just got in. Went straight downstairs to watch TV. He's more upset about the downsizing than he's letting on."

"I'll go look in on him."

"Don't you worry your dad about this. He's got enough on his plate right now without you adding to it. You hear me?"

I hear you. Dad always comes first.

16

I head down the stairs slowly, past all the maps Dad has papered the wall with—maps of places he's never been. Laughter blares from the TV. The scent of glue and paint rises up to greet me; he must be working on his model soldiers. I peer through the banister. Dad isn't watching the screen or working on his soldiers; he's holding his face in his hands, his shoulders shaking.

I take a step back. I've only seen Dad cry once in my life—the night he found out about the abuse. My legs wobble as if I'm ill.

I don't know whether to go back upstairs and pretend I never saw him or to let him know I'm here. I turn and sneak back up the stairs, then thump back down them as noisily as I can. "Dad! Hey Dad, where are you?" I pause at the corner, give him another few seconds to compose himself, then head into the rec room.

Dad's sitting up—his glasses back on, his face composed. Scattered on the table next to him are the bits and pieces of his model soldiers—arms and legs and torsos— ready to be glued together, and little jars of acrylic paint.

Dad turns down the volume on the TV and sets a soldier's head down on the table. "There's my girl! You're always so busy, I feel like I never get to see you any more."

He holds out his arms. I lean down to hug him, then flop beside him on the sagging couch and kiss his rough cheek. Dad chucks my chin with his strong hand. "How have you been holding up?"

I hear the footsteps in my mind again. I clench my hand until the scabbing wounds part, the pain jagged. "I'm okay." I look at his watery, reddened eyes and his blotchy neck, and I want to ask how he is. But I know I can't—not without him realizing I saw him cry.

Dad searches my eyes. "You sure?"

I pick at a tear in my jeans. "It's been hard lately, but nothing I can't handle."

"I know you're strong, honey. You don't have to prove it to me."

"I wasn't, I was—" *Trying to protect you.*

Dad shakes his head. "I know you think you always have to put up a front for your mom and me. I don't know where you get that from—"

From you guys!

"But you don't have to, Kendra. We're your parents. We want to be there for you."

Maybe you *do. Mom sure doesn't.*

Dad rubs his jaw. "I know you must be upset about the idea of moving—"

"It's not that, Dad." I pull away from him. "It's about leaving therapy and my friends. I need them right now."

"I know you do." Dad bows his head. "And you deserve it. It's just…." His voice trails off.

"It's okay, Dad. Mom told me. But listen—I can pay for the sessions myself. I just have to be able to get to them!"

"And that means you don't want to move."

I nod, hope rising inside me.

"I'm sorry, Kendra, but that's something I can't control. I can't pay the mortgage, and—"

"I thought you guys paid that off years ago?"

Dad looks startled. "We did. But when things started looking bad at work, I took out another mortgage. Thought I'd start up my own business—but that didn't work out. I'm just a damned failure, any way you look at it."

I've never heard him talk like this. It scares me. "You're not a failure, Dad."

"I am. My daughter needs therapy, and I can't even provide it for her."

I don't know what to say any more.

Dad laughs feebly. "Here I am, gabbing away, when I should be listening to you. That therapist of yours—you really feel she's helping you?"

"Yeah, I do."

"And you think it's important to keep seeing her?"

"Yes. I told you, Dad, I can pay for the sessions."

"But you can't pay the mortgage. Look, I'll go to the bank again, see if I can't work something out. Okay? I don't want to move, either. Your mother and I were married here. I ever tell you that? We were so young and so in love—"

I cross my legs. *I don't want to hear this.*

Dad stops, clears his throat. "I'll talk to the bank to-morrow. Now, you go upstairs and get some sleep. Leave the worrying to your mom and me."

As if I could.

17

I wake up feeling like I haven't slept. My eyes ache, my mouth tastes funky, and I feel sluggish. I want to roll over and go back to sleep. But then I think of Meghan and get myself to school.

Meghan finds me at my locker before the bell rings. "I'm serious about my offer," she says. "But you'd better be sure you want it. Living with my mom is no picnic."

I wonder if the bruise on her neck's faded yet. I touch her arm gently. "I know."

Meghan kicks at the floor. "You wanna hang out at lunch?"

"Of course!"

I think about Meghan in every class. I try to make her the *only* thing I think about. Because right behind her smile and her amber smell is the fear that I'll lose Carolyn. And beneath that, the sound of those footsteps keeps echoing through me, like a threat.

In every class, I dread opening my backpack, but each time, there's nothing new. I touch the blade in my pocket, needing to know it's there. I just have to get through the next two classes, and then Meghan will be with me, obliterating everything else.

Mr. Blair comes to stand beside me. He's staring down at my math paper. I follow his gaze. I've drawn hands in the margins of the page. *His* hands—reaching, grabbing like claws.

I shove my math book on top of the drawing, covering it. Mr. Blair makes a sound deep in his throat.

I stiffen. Is it *him*?

"I'd like to talk to you after class," he says, quietly.

I nod, not looking at him. I just sit there. clutching my pencil until he moves away. Then I scribble over the hands so hard I tear holes right through the paper.

I watch Mr. Blair as he leans over to talk to other students, his dark hair close to their heads, his eyes hidden behind his glasses. He leans a little closer to the girls, like they're flowers he wants to smell. My stomach clenches and unclenches.

I stare at his hands, trying to get a good look at them, but they're too far away, and I can't watch him long, in case he's the one.

The bell rings. Everyone scrambles up from their desks, scraping back chairs and shoving books into bags. They head for the door in a crush of bodies, and I want to leave with them, walk out like I've forgotten he asked me to stay. But I stay frozen in my seat, because he's a teacher. I stay because it might be *him*. And if there's one thing I know *he* enjoys, it's overpowering someone and watching them beg.

"Kendra." Mr. Blair comes to stand next to me. When

I don't look at him, he sits down at the desk beside me, his long legs splayed awkwardly beneath. His body odor fills my nostrils, making me want to gag.

"Is there anything you want to talk about?" he asks.

Nope. I shake my head hard.

"Because if there is, I'm here to listen. Maybe I can even help."

I look up at him quickly. "Who says I need help?"

His blue-grey eyes blink behind his glasses. "You seemed to be—blossoming—for a while," he says, smoothing his hand over his mustache. "But recently you've grown more preoccupied. Withdrawn."

His hot breath on my cheek. "I'll kill you if you tell."

Students from the next class are already filing into the room. Mr. Blair leans closer.

I shiver.

"If there's anything I can help you with—anything," he says, "I'd like to." He pauses, like he's waiting for me to answer him. But what am I supposed to say? *Gee, Mr. Blair, thanks so much for offering to let me confide in you, but I can't because you might be the man who sexually abused me?*

"I'd like you to consider seeing one of the guidance counselors," he says.

I stand. "Don't need to. I've got a therapist. Can I go now?"

He looks at me like he wants to say something else, but instead, he hands me a hall pass.

18

Lunch takes forever to come. I watch the minute hand of the wall clock tick its slow way around. Five minutes. Ten. A half hour. Then, finally, the bell rings and we're released.

There's no one at Meghan's locker, and I wonder if she's changed her mind. But then she's there beside me, her smile so beautiful I don't think I can paint it.

"Let's go sit on the hill."

That's Meghan all over—defiantly staking out her space, not even caring that it faces the teachers' parking lot.

We walk up together and sit under a tree. I love the feeling of being cut off from the rest of the school, with the back of the building separating us from the noise of the others. There are enough trees and grass on this little hill to make it feel like an oasis, except for the odd teacher who walks to a car or comes out to smoke.

Meghan pulls food out of her backpack: a bag of salt and vinegar chips, a pack of cupcakes, and a can of cola. It looks delicious—and totally unhealthy. My mom would freak.

"That's your lunch?"

Meghan narrows her eyes. "Yeah. So? What's yours?"

"Same thing my mom packs for me every day." I roll my eyes. "A tempeh and alfalfa sprouts sandwich, an organic apple, carrot sticks, one super-healthy cookie, and a juice box."

Meghan snorts. "Your mom packs your lunch?"

"It's a real thing with her. Makes her feel like a good parent, I guess."

"My mom hasn't packed my lunch since I was six. I remember coming home crying—I was starving because she'd forgotten to give me anything—and she gave me a wallop across the face. Told me to grow up."

"I'm sorry," I say softly.

"Hey, I'm not tellin' you so you'll cry—I'm tellin' you so you'll shut up about my crapola lunch." She laughs, her voice full of pain.

I want to hug her, but I don't dare.

Meghan looks at my lunch again, almost like she envies it.

"Wanna trade?" I say.

"Naw. You wouldn't like this shit."

"You kidding?" I laugh. "I *love* junk food."

We switch lunches, tearing into the food like we haven't eaten for days. Sugar buzzes through me, making me feel excited, happy. I lick the chocolate off my fingers, then wash it all down with the cola. "We should do this again."

"Fine by me." Meghan stretches out on the grass, her suntanned legs long beneath her shorts, her chest gently rising and falling.

Meghan squints up at me. "Whatcha looking at?"

"Nothing."

"You were so! Tell me!" She wrestles me to the grass. We tickle each other, laughing and screeching until we're tired.

I lie back against the prickly grass, and she moves closer, then leans her head against my shoulder. I wait for her to realize she's leaning on me, wait for her to move away, but she stays there, her hair close to my nose. I can smell her, a scent of flowers and amber and cigarettes.

Her head feels so good next to mine. I close my eyes and breathe her in. The sun is warm on my face, on my whole body, making me sleepy. Meghan's arm falls heavily across my stomach; I feel it rise and fall with my breath. I want this moment to stretch on and on. I think I'm starting to love her.

I snap my eyes open, stare up at the bright sky until it hurts. I can't fall in love with Meghan. She likes boys. I'll just get my heart broken—again. But I can't shut down how happy I feel around her.

I don't dare move; I hardly dare to breathe. I love her lying on me like this, so trusting. I want to protect her, to keep her from getting hurt. The feeling's so strong, I almost clutch her to me.

I wonder if this is what all survivors do—fall in love with someone they can't have. But Carolyn's got someone she loves, so there goes that theory.

"What're you thinking?" Meghan asks, lifting her head to look at me.

"Nothing."

"Come on, tell me." Meghan swats me.

I laugh, holding up my hands.

"You lezzies getting at it again?" a voice says. A guy's voice.

Meghan springs upright. "F-off, Tyler."

I sit up, heat washing over me like a sickness. It was so beautiful before Tyler came and ruined it. But of course it couldn't last. Nothing good ever does.

"What do you want?" Meghan asks him.

I can't look at her—can't bear to, so I look at him instead: curly black hair, full mouth, muscled arms. Meghan always picks good-looking guys. And all of them fall for her, just the way I have.

"I need you, Meghan," Tyler says.

Meghan sighs. "Again? What is it with you guys?"

"Come on, Meggie," Tyler says. "You know you're the only one I want."

I have to shut down how I feel about her. I can't believe I let it go this far.

Meghan touches my arm, and I feel her warmth right through my sleeve. "Catch you later, okay?"

"Sure." I smile hard.

Meghan looks at me, her eyes intense. But I can't read what they say.

19

I watch Meghan go, pulling Tyler after her. She seemed to be looking for something from me, but I don't know what it was, whether she wanted a reaction or a reason to stay. I laugh at myself, but still I wonder.

Loneliness wraps around me. Then the footsteps come rushing back, echoing through me again. My thoughts jump between the man who raped me and Meghan, between what I don't want and what I can't have. It's like the one hurt brings up the other, each making the other worse, until I want to scream.

The bell rings. I trudge down the hill and into the school. Next period is art, but I can't make myself care. People rush past, knocking into me, and I let them. It's not like paint can fix this. My feet drag along the floor like my thoughts—my abuser, Meghan, my abuser, Meghan. And now Mrs. Archer is in my head, too. Mrs. Archer, who saw me freak out; Mrs. Archer, who saw the drawing I never should have made. I'm afraid to face her, afraid to look into her eyes and see the pity I know will be there.

She won't see me as a talented student any more, as a

kid she likes; now she'll see me as a messed–up, damaged student who happens to like art. I'll be a student she has to be careful around. A student she pities.

The halls are empty. I touch the warm blade in my pocket and pinch the edge against my skin. There's hardly anyone left in the halls. I step up my pace.

The classroom door's already closed. I inch it open and slink in. Everyone turns to look, and I want to duck back out. Mrs. Archer pauses, nods at me, then goes back to telling the class the assignment. I creep over to my work-bench and shrug off my backpack. Then I plunk myself down, slamming my backpack down beside me.

Mrs. Archer didn't frown at me, didn't warn me not to be late, didn't even ask me for a pass. Already, she's treating me different from the others. And now I've got to sit through two whole periods with her.

I hook my legs under my stool and pick at the gouged wooden table. I knew it would mess things up being in art therapy with her. I should have said something, but I wanted to reassure her, wanted her to keep liking me—and now I've lost even that. I miss the connection between us, the warmth we used to have.

Mrs. Archer hovers behind me. "Kendra, get your supplies out, please. Let's get to work."

I slouch over to the counter without looking at her, then grab paint, brushes, and paper, not even caring what I take. I plunk them back down at my place, open a tube, and smear burnt umber and olive green over my paper. I push it around without watering it down; it's all muddy and dark, just like I feel inside.

People are laughing and talking while they work. I don't usually hear them; normally, everything disappears when I paint. But I hear them now. I want to yell at them to shut up.

Mrs. Archer comes up beside me again. "Kendra—is something wrong?"

"Why would anything be wrong?" I smile like a hyena.

"Well, if you're sure." Mrs. Archer looks at me, hesitating.

"I'm sure."

She leaves and I breathe easier. But I still can't paint. Nothing's coming. I'm afraid to let anything out on the paper, afraid to let her see the pain, the terror, the shadows that grip me.

Thirty minutes tick by—and all I've got is a ruined piece of watercolor paper.

Mrs. Archer comes back again and sits down beside me. "Kendra," she says quietly, "what's wrong?"

"Nothing's wrong, all right?" I say it too loud. People turn to look.

"Back to work, everyone. Class is almost over." Mrs. Archer leans closer. "Is this about the . . . group that we're both in? On Thursdays? Because if that's what's upsetting you, I'll leave it."

My eyes burn. I look up at her. She's watching me in that kind way she does. Like she actually cares what I think— what I feel. "That's okay," I say. "You don't have to do that."

"But I will, if it makes you uncomfortable. I don't want to encroach on your space there."

I twist the lid on the paint tube, on and off, on and off. I have to ask. "Do you see me differently now?"

"Differently? What do you mean?" Mrs. Archer's forehead wrinkles.

"Messed up. A head case. A total screw-up."

Mrs. Archer stares at me, her mouth opening. "No, Kendra. I see you as strong. Courageous. An example for others." She presses her hand flat against the workbench, her eyes bright like she's holding in tears. "You stood up for someone else. And you faced things that hurt you. That shows me your strength—and your courage even more."

"But don't you even—I mean, you didn't know someone had—hurt me . . . until that group."

Mrs. Archer looks down at her hands. She folds them, then unfolds them. She looks back at me. "Kendra—I knew from your art. It's so intense. And I knew from your behavior that you'd been through something painful, something that hurt you deeply. That's why I encourage you so much—besides your being the most talented student I've ever had. I think you've got to get out whatever's hurting you through your art, so it doesn't twist you up inside."

She looks at me like she's trying to see if I'm listening. "And if my being in the art therapy group stops you from expressing yourself, I'll leave. I care more about you than about my training; I can get that any time."

I want to cry—and to laugh. Mrs. Archer still likes me!

"Don't leave," I say. "I want you there." I smile at her, as much as I *can* smile. I'm ashamed of how I acted—but I feel closer to her, too. And if I hadn't said anything, I'd never have known that things are all right between us. I'd never have known that it was *my* shame and fear I was seeing, not hers.

20

"I'm so glad," Mrs. Archer says as she stands. "You're a delight to work with." I wonder how I could ever have thought she was judging me. She's so much better than that.

She dismisses the class. I carry my sketchbook up to the front. When I'm sure no one is looking, I pull out the X-acto knife and slip it back onto the table, behind the paintbrushes. I look around fast, but Mrs. Archer is still talking with a student and everybody else is busy gathering their stuff and leaving.

I let out my breath. I didn't feel right with a knife that wasn't mine. Especially one from Mrs. Archer's room.

Now that I've put it back, I can focus on art class. I choose my paints and paper carefully, humming under my breath. I know what I want to paint: Meghan.

I paint her over and over, but I can't seem to get it right; I can't seem to capture that tenderness and vulnerability that sits in her eyes, behind all the toughness. Mrs. Archer smiles at my work when she passes by, and I know she thinks it's good. But it's not good enough for me. I want it to be perfect.

I put my work away reluctantly at the end of class. I don't want to stop until I've got it right. Even in science and English, I'm still trying to get on paper that look Meghan gets in her eyes. I draw Meghan tender and sweet, strong and fierce. I draw her playful and happy, the way she's been with me. And I write her name, over and over, next to mine.

I don't want to stop thinking about her. Every time I stop, dark thoughts crowd me and prickle my mind—the footsteps, Dad losing his job, therapy ending—and I can't go there, not without wanting to cut. So I just keep thinking about Meghan, and feel warm and good all over.

When the last bell rings, I head over to Meghan's locker and wait. I silently rehearse what I want to say, trying for casual, spur of the moment. Lockers slam shut around me, and people call out good-byes to each other. The halls are emptying fast.

When I look up, Meghan's heading toward me, Tyler attached to her like a leech. I ram my hands into my pockets.

"Hey," Meghan says. "What're you doing here?"

I can't tell if she's glad to see me or not. "I was just . . ."

Tyler's looking at me like I'm a joke.

I stare at the floor, then up at Meghan again. Her eyes urge me on. I swallow. "You want to hang out this weekend?"

Tyler howls. "Told you she's got the hots for you!"

My cheeks are hot as a slap. I wish I'd never said anything.

Meghan plucks Tyler's arm off her waist and shoves him away. "Grow up, Tyler." She turns back to me. "Sounds good. Saturday morning? First thing? I'll call you."

"Great!" Happiness spreads to my belly like warmth from a cup of hot chocolate. I race down the hall away from her before she can change her mind.

I leap down the stairs, three at a time, using the banister as a pole vault; it's like I'm flying. I swing myself off the last few steps and slam right into a hard body—right into Mr. Blair.

I scramble away from him. "Oh my God, I'm so sorry!"

Mr. Blair smooths out his shirt. "Hey, that's all right." His face softens as he looks at me over the top of his glasses. "It's good to see you having fun."

I stand there, waiting for a reprimand. But Mr. Blair just pushes his glasses back up his nose, then leaves. I can't tell if he really meant what he said, whether the warmth I saw in his eyes was real or not.

His hand gripping my wrist. His lips against my ear. "I will kill you if you tell."

I stare at the space where Mr. Blair was, waiting for more shadows to wrap around me, but nothing comes. *Maybe he's not the one.*

I shrug and step out into the warmth of the afternoon, a soft breeze brushing against my face. I flash to Meghan and me on the hill, sitting in the sun.

I see her tomorrow!

Excitement fizzes through me, lifting me up until I want to run all the way home.

21

Mom's not at the door to greet me. *Maybe she's finally letting me be.*

I walk in and climb the back stairs to the kitchen, expecting to smell oil paint and turpentine, but there's a heaviness in the house instead. Mom's sitting there, drinking chamomile tea, a pile of crumpled–up tissues on the table in front of her. She gets up abruptly when she hears me, her mug rocking against the table. "Kendra, I want to talk to you."

I cross my arms over my chest and wait.

"Your father got a strange call at work this morning. From his friend, Terry Blair. Your math teacher."

My hands grow cold.

"Your dad thought Terry was calling about their hunting trip, but instead, Terry was calling about you. He says you've been acting strange lately. Different. Maybe depressed. He's worried about you."

I'll bet he is. "I'm fine."

"Mr. Blair didn't seem to think so. He wants us to come in for a conference. He thinks something might be worrying you."

"Nothing's worrying me!" *Damn it, why is this happening?* "Believe me, I'm fine!"

Mom bites her lip, staining her teeth with lipstick. "He said he thought he saw something strange in your pocket—something that shouldn't be there." *Oh, God!* My chest aches with held-in air. *He can't have seen the blade. He can't have!*

"Kendra," Mom says, and she's crying now, "you're not thinking of suicide, are you?"

"Of course not!" I force a laugh. "That's absurd."

"Even so—I need to check your pockets. I need to know . . . ."

I can't breathe properly, can't suck in air. I drop my backpack to the floor, lick my lips. "Mom—" I try to smile, but I know I'm grimacing. "This is all a mistake. I was a little down today; I admit it. I probably flunked my history test. That must have been what Mr. Blair was picking up on." *One little lie isn't so bad.* "But I'm not suicidal. I haven't thought about it for months." *Not since I've been seeing Carolyn.*

"And what he thought he saw in my pocket—" *Is still there—* "was something I borrowed from the art room, to cut some matting. I meant to return it today and forgot." *Okay, two little lies.*

I reach for my blade and pull it out, trying to look nonchalant. I'm glad I always clean it off after I cut, glad there's nothing to give away what I use it for, except a slight discoloration.

"But a blade, Kendra? Why would you have a blade in your pocket? And one without a handle?"

"It made it easier to carry. And I just forgot about it. I'll return it on Monday, I promise." *I don't know if I'm making sense. I don't even care; I just want her to believe me.*

"But that's dangerous. You shouldn't be carrying it around like that."

"I know how to handle mat knives, Mom. I respect them, believe me." I tuck it back into my pocket.

Mom's looking at me like she's not sure what to think.

Sweat trickles down my sides. "Come on, Mom…. Has Carolyn called you? Have you heard any worried reports from her?"

"No, but—"

"Mr. Blair doesn't know what he's talking about. I tell Carolyn everything. There's nothing wrong, okay?" I hug her fast.

Mom clings to me. "Your dad and I were so worried about you."

"Well, there's nothing to worry about."

Mom pulls back and looks me deep in the eyes. "You're telling me the truth?"

"Yes, I'm telling you the truth," I say. *And I am. Cutting isn't anything to worry about. Now, the footsteps and the man coming after me—that's something else again.*

The kettle screams, and Mom switches the burner off. "Your dad thinks we should set up a session with Carolyn, to find out what you haven't been telling us."

"You can't do that. My sessions are private!"

"How else are we supposed to find out what's going on? You never talk to us."

"I'm not supposed to!" I want to rip my arm open and

let the blood gush out. "That's what teenagers do; they grow away from their parents!"

"Not like this. We're worried about you, Kendra. You're so unhappy. And if you won't talk to us, we'll have to find some other way of getting the information. We have the right to know what's going on. Carolyn said as much to me."

And you pay the bills. I can't believe this is happening. But money talks. I just didn't think Carolyn would be like that.

I want to slash my arm as hard and as fast as I can. But I can't give in; I can't risk Mom finding out.

I shove my hand into my pocket, touch the sharp edge of the blade, then the smooth warmth of the stone. I won't let myself panic. Not until I talk to Carolyn and find out what's going on. Because Mom doesn't always tell the truth.

22

I shut the door to my room, take out my cell, and punch the speed dial button for Carolyn.

Her voicemail switches on.

I throw my phone onto my bed, pace over to my window, then come back again. The light on my alarm clock blinks at me like a warning signal. I yank out the plug.

I can't keep the blade in my pocket any more—not now that Mom's seen it—but I have to have it on me. *Need* to have it. I pull the blade out, pressing it into the tips of my fingers. I don't draw blood; but just knowing I can helps me breathe.

Then I roll up my pant leg and tug open my sock. The blade slides in easily and lies against my skin, flat and warm. I snap the sock against my leg. Then I roll my jeans back down. Perfect.

I try Carolyn again. No answer, still. *Calm. I must stay calm.* The blade calls to me, screaming for me to use it, but I can't risk Mom barging in on me.

I sit down at my desk, getting out my paints and paper

with shaking hands. Watercolor this time, not gouache. I don't know what I'm going to paint until Meghan's face starts to appear beneath my brush. I lose myself in the act of stroking paint onto paper, letting the pigments spread beneath the bristles.

It's only when I dab the last detail onto her face, add the brightness of her eyes, that I lean back and look at what I've created. It's Meghan laughing, golden sunlight all around her like an aura. Flowers sprout from her skin, and butterflies rest on her head and shoulders. There are no shadows, no hidden corners of pain—just happiness and light.

I sit back. I don't think I've ever painted something without the pain leaking through; it feels good.

The painting is almost as beautiful as Meghan—one of the best I've ever done. But would she like it if I gave it to her? Or was she just being polite at the Java Cup? The mistakes I've made start to jump out at me: the brush strokes that are too heavy, the clumsiness of the flowers, the way her smile doesn't look quite right.

"Kendra? Can I come in?"

I turn to see Mom in my doorway.

What am I supposed to say? No? "Yeah, sure." I shove my painting on top of the filing cabinet beneath my desk, and cover my brushes under some papers.

Mom sits down on the edge of my bed. "I found these in your bag," she says, holding out some notes ripped from my binder. No, not notes. The sketches of Meghan I did in my classes.

"You went through my stuff?"

"I was worried about you."

"Well, don't be. My friendship with Meghan is a good thing. You don't have to try to fix it." *Or ruin it.*

"I don't want to fix it, I just—"

"You what?" *I can't believe you think you can go through my stuff.*

"I just wondered if you've really thought this through. You're obsessed with this—" She looks at the sketches, "This Meghan girl—but what you decide now could affect your entire life. I know you're still struggling with what that man did to you—"

"What he did to me has nothing to do with this!"

Mom squeezes her hands together. "Maybe you don't think so now, but in a few years—"

"No, Mom. Not ever." Nothing as beautiful as Meghan and me could ever come from something as awful as abuse.

"Well, if it's not the sexual abuse that made you this way, then what is it? Help me; I'm trying to understand."

"I never asked you to." *I can't believe we're having this conversation.*

Sadness creases Mom's face. "I know you didn't. You didn't even tell me about her."

Because I didn't think you'd be able to hear it. Didn't think you could be happy for me. Guilt presses against my heart: Did I misjudge her? "I love her, Mom. She makes me happy."

"The way Sarah made you happy? And then so un-happy that you wanted to die?"

I stare at her, my eyes stretching wide. *You knew. You*

must have known all along, and you never said anything. Not about the pills. And not about Sarah. "That wasn't about Sarah. That was about the memories I was having." *It was about the pain I couldn't hold.*

"Whatever it was, I'm sure this homosexuality didn't make it any easier. All I'm saying is, maybe you can talk to Carolyn about this. Make sure you aren't becoming a homosexual because of the abuse."

Homosexual. The way she says the word feels like a fist in my mouth, like it's something hurtful, something disgusting. She never talked about even the abuse like this.

"Did you even listen to me, Mom? Did you hear what I said?"

"Of course I did."

"She makes me feel *good*. She makes me feel happy."

Mom twists her ring around her finger. "This is all my fault. If only I'd spent more time with you when you were little. If only I didn't ask Sandy to look after you—"

"Sandy didn't make me a lesbian!" I clench my teeth. "How can you be so hypocritical? Sandy's your friend— and you don't try to change *him!*"

"He's not my daughter!"

But I am. Great. I can see where this is going, now. "I don't want to change, Mom. I don't need to."

She bows her head and goes silent.

I lean forward. "Please—can't you just try to understand? You say I never talk to you. But how can I, if you won't even accept who I am? I need you to do that, Mom. I need you to accept me."

Mom nods and looks at me, her eyes shiny with tears.

"I think I'll need some time. But you're right, Kendra; you don't need to change. And you shouldn't. Not for me and not for anyone else. That's something I've always admired about you—your passion for things you care about. I wish I could be more like that."

"I—thank you." Sometimes she surprises me.

"I'm not saying I understand, yet. But I'll try. Sandy's a good man and a good friend, and once I got past him being gay, I could see that. People will see that in you, too."

Okay... at least she's trying.

Mom gets up. "You're my daughter, Kendra, and I love you. I know you sometimes find that hard to believe, but I do. And I want you to be happy. So if you feel this strongly about Meghan, then I'll support you."

She reaches out to hug me. I hug her back. For the first time in a long time, I feel like Mom loves me. Or at least she's trying to.

23

I hear Mom walk quickly down the hall, like she can't wait to get away from me. I can hardly believe that she admires something in *me*. She's never said that before.

Her bedroom door squeaks, and I know she's gone to lie down, worn out by our conversation. Or maybe by all the emotion she tries to lock inside of her. I hear her shoes hit the floor, hear her sigh. I try not to let guilt swallow me up.

I stare out my window. There are shadows in the backyard that the moon doesn't light up—shadows that move and flit through the night the way they flit through my mind. They're probably just raccoons, rooting through our garbage, but I can't help thinking about the footsteps following me home. *I wish it was Monday already. Wish I was in Carolyn's office. I have so much to tell her.*

I run my hand through my hair. *No, I wish it was Saturday and I was with Meghan, not stuck here in my room.*

The side door slams. "I'm home!" There's the creak of the bed as Mom gets up, the shuffle of her slippers going down the hall, and then her voice, thin and high. Dad's voice rumbles back.

I dive into bed, switch out my light, and pull the pillow over my head.

Their voices rise and fall, then there's quiet. Footsteps thump down the hall.

"Kendra?" Dad says softly.

Maybe if I pretend I'm asleep, he'll go away. I keep my eyes closed, make my breathing slow and steady.

"Kendra, I know you're awake."

Shit. I lift the pillow off my head and turn over. Dad's in my doorway, hands shoved into his pockets the way he does when he's nervous.

"Your mother and I are worried about you. I know you've been having a rough time lately—"

Not another talk. I can't stand it. "I'm fine, Dad. I already told Mom that."

"You don't look fine."

"Well, I am. Why can't you both just stop worrying about me?"

"It's part of our job." Dad clears his throat. "Do you think this lesbian thing could have anything to do with, you know, the sexual abuse?"

"God, not you, too! Can't you leave it alone? It's not the problem you guys think it is."

"It's not that simple, Kendra. Saying there's no problem doesn't mean there isn't one."

"Why is it a problem? Because if I like girls, I'll be different from you?"

"No. Because if you choose to be lesbian, you choose

a hard road. People are afraid of what's different. They're afraid of what they don't know. And people can get pretty mean when they're afraid."

I'm not sure it's a choice. The way I was drawn to Sarah, the way I feel about Meghan—it's so strong. "Is that what got Mom all twisted up? She's afraid of me being different?"

Dad jingles the change in his pockets. "I guess so. She's afraid of how other people will treat you. She's afraid you're making things harder for yourself. She's worried that on top of everything you've been through, this will be too much."

"Too much for me or for her?"

"Good question."

He's really listening to me, taking me seriously. *Why can't Mom and I talk like this? Maybe it's because she doesn't know me, not really.*

Dad's still jingling the change in his pockets. I've never seen him so nervous.

I rub my eyes. "Is there something else you wanted to talk about?"

"Yes." Dad clears his throat again. "This knife Terry saw. Um, I mean, Mr. Blair. You're returning it to school on Monday, right? That's the last we'll see of it?"

"Absolutely. You'll never see it again." *I'll make sure of that.*

"Good, good. Well, sleep well, Kendra." Dad hesitates, walks in, then kisses my forehead. "I love you, kitten. We'll get through this. Just hang in there."

"Yeah. Night, Dad."

Dad turns and walks down the hall, his footsteps heavy and slow. I hear the creak of the bed again, and then their voices murmuring.

I want to tell them to stop worrying, but I can only say it so many times and they don't seem to listen, anyway.

I stare up at the ceiling, thinking I won't be able to sleep. But I close my eyes, and I do.

24

I avoid Mom and Dad all morning, and wait for Meghan to call. I clean my desk, roll up the painting I did of Meghan and slide it into a cardboard tube, and check my cell. I look at my homework, put the books back down again, make a few doodles, and stare out the window until the phone rings.

Seconds after we hang up, I'm out of there with the tube in my hand. "I'm going to meet a friend. Back later!"

The door slams behind me. I start off down the street, pretending I can't hear Mom calling after me. My feet hardly touch the sidewalk. The air smells of freshly mown grass and flowers. The sun is warm. *And Meghan is waiting for me!* I laugh out loud.

The closer I get, the tighter my stomach gets. I toss the tube from one hand to the other. I don't know any more if the painting is such a good idea. Maybe she'll get weirded out. Maybe it'll look like I'm coming on too strong.

The back of my head prickles with that being-watched feeling. I whirl around—but there's no one there who could be him. Just a woman walking a dog, a guy on roller blades, and two girls giggling together.

His hand, gripping my wrist. A handkerchief falling to the floor.

I pick up my pace until I'm almost running, but I can't shake the feeling that someone is watching me.

A car passes me slowly, rolling by like there's a shaky old driver behind the wheel. *Or someone who's tailing me.* I run until I reach the Saturday-morning shopping crowd; then I slow down and try to blend in. The air smells like coffee, fresh bread, and car exhaust.

Meghan's standing outside the Java Cup, looking like she's drawn all the sunshine to her skin. I want to hug her, but I don't know how to do it without looking stupid. So I hang back.

"Hey," she says, grinning like she's glad to see me.

"Hey, yourself." I grin back at her, then peek over my shoulder at the crowd.

There are lots of men now—husbands with their wives, men carrying children on their shoulders, businessmen talking on phones, men reading their newspapers and sipping their cappuccinos. I don't know where *he* is, if he's here at all. *He* could be sitting right outside the Java Cup, and I'd never know it.

"Everything okay?" Meghan asks.

No. But I want it to be. "You feel like taking a walk?"

"Sure." Meghan shrugs. "I'm easy."

We start off down the street. I love how Meghan can just go with things, how she doesn't get rattled by a change in plans—the way I would.

"What's in the tube?" she asks, reaching over and tapping it.

I breathe in the sweet smell of amber mixed with her sweat. "It's for you." I thrust the tube into her hands.

"For me?"

"Yeah." A nervous giggle, like a hiccup, pops out of my mouth.

Meghan pulls the lid off the tube, slips the paper partway out. "Hey—is this one of your paintings?"

"Yeah."

Meghan taps the painting back in, snaps the lid on. "Then I want to wait till we stop someplace. I wanna look at it proper."

She's treating my art like it's something special. I rub my sweaty hands on my jeans. Part of me wants her to just get it over with, and part of me really likes that she cares about my art enough to look at it slowly. That she cares about me.

Meghan bops me on the head with the tube. "Thank you," she says. "You shouldn't have."

"You don't even know what I painted."

"I know it's something good," she says firmly.

"It is."

I feel someone staring at me like they want to hurt me. I whirl around in a quick circle, but I can't see anyone watching us.

Meghan squints at me. "What's with you today? You act like someone's after you."

"Someone might be."

"Seriously?" Meghan stops walking.

A bicyclist rings his bell angrily at her.

"You don't like it, get off the sidewalk!" Meghan shouts, giving him the finger.

"Let's keep going, okay?" I say, touching her arm. "At least to the park."

I start walking, and Meghan joins me.

"But who's after you? What's going on?"

"*He's* after me. My abuser. At least, I *think* he is."

"You mean, the guy you don't remember?"

"Yeah." I try to laugh. "That MP3 player I gave you? That was from *him*. There was a note from him earlier, too. I'm sure *he's* been following me, trying to scare me." I look at her. "I know how this sounds, but I'm not making it up."

"I know you're not." Meghan frowns. "He shouldn't get away with this."

"Well, I can't exactly call the police. 'Hey, officer, I think someone's following me—but I don't know what he looks like, except for his hands. And, oh yeah, I think he's the guy who raped me when I was little.' That'd go over really well, wouldn't it?"

"Aw, cops. What do they do, anyway, except swagger around?" Meghan juts her chin out. "We can do better. He doesn't want you to know who he is, right? I say we turn around and yell out what he did to you. Make everyone turn and look. With two of us, he wouldn't dare try anything."

I go cold. "No! He said he'd kill me if I ever told."

"You've got to fight back somehow."

"But not like that."

25

I turn off the sidewalk and into the park. Leafy trees whisper in the wind, and birds call to each other from the branches. Even the air smells fresher, less like car exhaust, even though the cars are just a street away. I flop down on the grass, lean my head back against my hands, and look up at the green leaves and patches of blue sky.

Meghan flops down next to me. "We'll figure something out. Don't worry. You're not in this alone."

She's looking at me so intensely, I want to lean over and kiss her. Instead, I snatch the tube back and bop her on the head. "Aren't you going to open this?"

"Hey!" Meghan grabs the tube and bops me back.

I laugh, shielding my head.

She pulls the cap off and draws the painting out, unrolling it carefully. Then she sits there, staring at it.

I'm scared I've freaked her out, but when she looks at me, her eyes are shining.

"It's beautiful," she says. She leans over and kisses me on the cheek, lets her lips rest against my skin for a moment. "Thank you." Then she starts to cry.

I don't know what to do. I rub her back. "What is it?"

Meghan gulps. "No one's ever done anything like this for me before." She wipes her cheeks with her wrists. "It's so . . . romantic."

Romantic. The word echoes between us.

I keep my gaze on the ground, watch an ant crawl up a blade of grass. She can't mean it the way I think she does. There must be some other meaning for the word.

"Kendra?" Meghan reaches for my hand.

Our fingers touch, warmth exploding through me.

I jerk away. "But you—you like boys." My cheeks burn.

Meghan hunches over the painting. Her hair falls over her face, blocking my view. "I sleep with boys. There's a difference."

"You have sex with them . . . but you don't like them?"

Meghan looks up at me through the curtain of her hair. "Hey, I told you I was screwed up."

"You're not screwed up."

"Whatever." She looks away again and jabs the ground.

I want to touch her face, her hand; I want to reassure her.

She rips up a handful of grass, then throws it jerkily away. "I've always been turned on by girls. But I thought that if I slept with enough boys, I'd get it out of my system—start thinking like everyone else."

"And you haven't?" My voice is hoarse and deep. I almost don't recognize it.

"Nah." Meghan cups my face in her warm hands and kisses me.

Her lips are soft and wet against mine. I never knew it could feel so good. So beautiful.

Meghan pulls away, tears rolling down her cheeks.

"What's wrong?" I ask, my heart pounding in my ears.

She shakes her head, still crying. I wrap my arms around her, and she leans into me, pressing her face against my neck. I can feel her tears against my skin.

I wish I could take her sadness away. I hold her tighter. Meghan cries and cries. I don't know what to do, so I just keep holding her.

Meghan sniffs and laughs. "Sorry; I don't normally do this."

"It's okay. It helps get it out."

Meghan sits up, her shoulder still touching mine. She twists her leather bracelet around her wrist, the wood beads appearing, then disappearing. "Maybe I sleep with boys because I don't feel close to them. There's no way to get hurt."

"But there's no way to feel much love, either," I say. "Not when you're cut off like that."

"I know." Meghan shudders. "I could feel it—love, connection, something—with you. Kissing you was different. Don't be mad, Kendra. But I don't know if I'm ready to let someone in that much."

"I'm not mad," I say softly. "I can wait as long as it takes."

And I can. I will.

Because I love her.

26

Meghan smiles, lips puffy and vulnerable. "Let's just hold hands for a while."

I reach for her hand. It feels soft and strong at the same time. It feels right. Not like *his* hands.

I wrench my gaze from hers. I'd forgotten about being followed. I take a quick look at the people scattered around the park: the shoppers strolling along the sidewalk, the people sitting at the café across the street. But I don't see anyone watching us—watching me.

Meghan traces my hand with her fingers.

I shiver. Her fingers trail up to my wrist. I feel the ache in my arm and the heat from the wounds. *Can't let her see.*

I jerk away.

Meghan pulls me back, turning my arm over. "What's this?"

A small corner of white bandage pokes out from beneath my sleeve. I jerk away again, yank my sleeve farther down. "Nothing; it's nothing."

"I don't think it's nothing."

My heart is beating too fast. I never thought this would

actually happen—someone finding out. I've been so careful. But Meghan sees me, and I don't know whether to be scared or happy.

"Kendra." Meghan takes hold of my hand again, clasps it in both of hers. "Don't you trust me?"

"Yes, but—" I bite my lip. "If I show you, you can't tell anyone. Promise?"

"I promise."

Trusting her scares me, but that's what love is all about. At least I think it is.

I undo the button on my sleeve, rolling it up to show the gauze beneath, greyish white and bloodstained.

"Jesus," Meghan says, her voice choked with tears.

"Don't look yet. Just give me a minute."

Meghan closes her eyes.

I turn away from her. I don't want her to see me do this. I unroll the gauze and stuff it in my pocket. Then I tug at the edge of one of the white pads. It sticks painfully to my arm, pulling at the skin. I grit my teeth.

There's no pain when I cut, just the easing of fear inside me. The pain comes after, when I'm finished. But it's a fast, clean pain that shuts down everything I need it to. I expect it; I even want it. But this pain feels messy and slow, and it's not strong enough to do anything but make me hurt. And I don't like hurting.

I hold my breath and yank hard. The pad comes off, taking pieces of brownish yellow scabs with it, leaving open, bloody wounds. I yank the second pad off and turn around.

Meghan's eyes are already open. I slowly stretch my arm out toward her.

I can hear her breath catch in her throat.

The wounds I made the other night are scabbing over, ugly soft yellow crusts working to join the puffy, reddened flesh back together. My arm is a grotesque patchwork of unbroken flesh, hardening scabs, and shiny new red strips of skin—and now, small, bloody mouths where some scabs got ripped off.

Meghan covers her mouth. "Why did you do this?"

"Why do you sleep around?" I snap—and then wish I could take it back. I reach out my hand. "I'm so sorry; I didn't mean that."

"It's all right."

"No, it's not…." I look at the ground. "Damn. I was scared you were judging me."

"I'm not. And you're not the one who deserves to be hurt, Kendra. *He* is."

"That's not why. I'm not punishing myself. Not most of the time, anyway. I cut because it helps me."

Meghan frowns, looking puzzled, and I know she wants to understand.

"Cutting stops the memories when I need them to stop. It bleeds the pain away when I can't take it any more. It gives me relief. Lets me breathe."

"It numbs you?"

"Yeah. Emotionally, anyway. At least for a while."

Meghan moistens her lips. "I understand that. Fucking boys numbs me, too. I just wish you didn't have to hurt yourself this way."

"Yeah." I twist my shoelace into knots. "Still think you want to get involved with me someday? I'm more messed up than you know."

"I like you for you. This doesn't change how I feel. Besides, all I see here is pain. And that's something we both know a lot about."

I can't speak, or I'll burst into tears. I take the gauze out of my pocket.

Meghan stops me. "Can I touch them? The healed ones, I mean," she asks softly.

Her eyes are a deep, clear green, and there's nothing hard in them. I lean closer, and she runs her fingers over my arm, staying away from the open wounds. The scars are like a crazy quilt, running in all directions—some are raised like welts, some are sunken beneath. Some spread across my skin like narrow leaves, while others are slender nips in my flesh. They shine brightly where nothing should, taking my breath away.

I stare at the bright red welts of skin. I knew they were there. I'd watched the open wounds change to scabs, then the scabs eventually disappear or be torn off to leave these red marks of pain. But I hadn't thought about them beyond that. I hadn't thought about them being permanent.

"I almost envy you your scars," Meghan says. "They're something visible, something you can point to, to show how much you hurt. Something that lasts longer than a bruise. I don't have that."

"I never thought about it that way," I say slowly. "I guess they're like the marks *he* never left on my skin."

Meghan runs her fingers over my scars again. No one's ever touched them before. No one's ever seen them, except me. It doesn't feel as shameful as I thought it would. It almost feels like a relief, to have someone know—and to have that person not judge me.

Meghan lets go of my arm.

I slap the pads back on and start rolling the gauze over my arm; it's awkward, working with only one hand.

"Let me do that," Meghan says. She takes the gauze from me and wraps my arm, her movements soft and gentle.

I feel almost taken care of. Like she cares about me, doesn't want to hurt it. Doesn't want to hurt me.

I roll my sleeve back down and button it tightly.

"I hate *him*," Meghan says, gripping her knees. "I hate him more than ever."

"Meghan—the cutting helps me. It really does."

"I know," she says with a sad smile. "I know."

She stands up, and we walk out of the park together, holding hands. Some people stare at us, but I don't care. I feel too happy.

"I had a good time with you today," Meghan says.

"I did, too."

We stop under a tree at the edge of the sidewalk. People pass in front of us, heading in and out of the Java Cup, carrying cups of coffee and bags of pastries.

I trace my shoe along the thick, ridged root of the tree. Its old, sturdy branches give us shade. Meghan leans toward me and kisses me softly on the lips. I tremble inside.

She pulls back. "Was that okay?"

"Of course!" I grin at her. "I love it."

"Even though I want to go slow?"

"You can take all the time you need," I say. "I want this to feel right for both of us."

Meghan touches my cheek. "I don't think you know how special you are—"

141

A boy on a skateboard skids to a stop in front of us. "Hey!"

We jump apart.

The boy—he can't be more than twelve, maybe thirteen—stands there with one hip jutting out, a sneer on his face. His spiky blond hair looks hard, like it has too much gel in it. "One of you Kendra Marshall?" he asks.

"Yeah," I say cautiously. "Why?"

"Got something for you," he says, pulling a narrow box out from under his arm.

"Who's it from?" I step back and away from him.

The boy shrugs. "Some guy in a suit. Paid me twenty bucks to give it to you."

It's *him*. It has to be. Dizziness whooshes through my head, and the sidewalk tilts crazily beneath me.

Meghan clenches her fists "What guy? Show me!"

"Uh-uh. Not until you take the package. That was the deal." He thrusts the package at me. I catch it reflexively. I want to throw it away from me, but instead I stand there clutching it, my hands shaking.

The boy starts to roll off on his skateboard.

Meghan grabs him by the arm. "Not so fast. Show me this guy."

"Hey—what you getting so upset about? And what's in it for me?"

"Knowing you did the right thing. That guy's harassing her."

"How was I supposed to know? He looked like a decent guy. Said it was a birthday present. He wanted to surprise her."

142

Meghan rolls her eyes. "And you believed him?"

"Hey—he gave me a twenty," the boy says, flicking the bill out of his pocket and smirking.

"Great." Meghan snatches the bill from him. "I'll give it back to you as soon as you show me the guy."

"That's not fair!"

"Show me. Then you'll get it back."

"All right, all right—" He picks up his skateboard and turns to look. "He's not there any more."

"Just show me where he was. And you can tell me what he looked like." She touches my arm. "I'll be right back. You okay for a minute?"

"Sure." My head feels so light and empty that it doesn't feel connected to the rest of my body. I watch them go off, then I look at the box. *He* found me again. *He* found me just like he said he would.

Even though I don't want to, even though I'm afraid to look, I'm tearing open the box as if my hands belong to someone else.

A single white handkerchief and a crudely sharpened palette knife lie nestled in red tissue paper. I feel a strange movement in my head, a kind of shifting. Then suddenly, desperately, I need to cut.

I burst through the doors of the Java Cup, run past the startled customers, my paintings jeering at me from the walls. I dash into the rest room, tear the blade from beneath my sock. Almost before I shut and lock the door, I slash myself over and over again, the blade slicing through me until the sink is splattered with blood.

I set the blade down with a clatter.

This is crazy.

I begin to shiver—great, bone-crushing shivers that come from deep inside. Images, like photos, keep appearing in my mind—of me cutting into my arm, of me slicing right through the veins in my wrist. I wonder how quickly I'll die, and whether it'll hurt much.

Die?

I pack toilet paper against my arm and sink to the cold floor. I can almost hear Carolyn asking what set this off.

"I'm so scared," I say, as if she's here to listen. "He's coming after me like he said he would!" My teeth chatter.

I reach up for my blade, the bloody toilet paper falling on the tiles. Shadows flash like lightning through my mind.

A door, snapping shut behind me. His hand, pressing my fingers around a knife. His breath against my cheek, against my ear.

"You will cut to keep silent. You will cut to forget. And if you tell, you will cut to kill yourself."

Then the shadows, the words are gone.

I lean back against the wall, shaken.

"It's okay." I breathe out, my lungs quivering. "He was trying to scare me, to keep me quiet. That's all."

What if you're wrong? a voice whispers inside me. *What if he tries to rape you again? Wouldn't it be better to die now, than to let that happen?*

I stare at the wet blade. It would be so easy to cut a little deeper—

"No!"

I throw the blade down. "I want to live."

Another flash.

Blinding light in my eyes. A handkerchief, falling to the floor. A large hand, gripping my wrist. A hand I think I recognize.

"Stop it, just stop it!" I scream. I slam the door of my mind on the image, shut my mind against the pain.

Carolyn. I've got to call Carolyn.

I fumble for my cell and pull it out of my pocket. My hands are shaking so much that I can barely flip open the phone. I speed dial Carolyn, not knowing what I'm going to say. I just know I need to hear her voice.

"Hello—"

"Carolyn!" I cry.

"You have reached the voicemail of Carolyn Fairchild. Please leave a message at the sound of the tone—"

I almost hang up, but I wait until the beep sounds, then clear my throat, trying not to sound as desperate as I feel. "Carolyn? It's Kendra. Something happened, and I really need to talk to you. He sent me another message—" My voice chokes off.

I hang up before I start sobbing. God, I'm a mess.

"Kendra! Kendra? Are you in there?" It's Meghan. She's pounding on the door. "Kendra, let me in!"

"Just a minute!" I stand up shakily, then wipe my blade and tuck it away.

"Open up the door—now!" Her voice grows fainter, like she's turned her head away. "Hey! Could I get some help over here? My friend's in trouble!"

"No, just hang on!" I yell. Hot blood curls down my arm in long, thin streams. I can't let her see me like this. I won't put her through that. I grab more toilet paper off the roll and press it tight against my arm.

"Kendra, open the door *now*! Or I'll get somebody to open it up!"

I can tell she means it.

I punch my thigh. I don't know what to do.

"Kendra!"

I turn the handle and open the door a crack, peeking out.

Meghan shoves her way past me, knocking my arm, and slams the door behind her. Then she notices the blood: "Oh, my God. Oh, my God!" It's everywhere—spattered on the floor and on the sink, wads of reddened toilet paper clumped on the tiles. Blood trickles down my arm.

"I didn't want you to see this," I say. My teeth are chattering again.

"But I did. I have. And you know what, Kendra? I'm not running away."

I don't know how she knows exactly the right thing to say, but it calms me and lets me take a breath.

"We've got to get you to a doctor," Meghan says.

I shake my head. "No doctor." There'd be no way I could hide my cutting if a doctor saw it.

"But you can't leave your arm like this! You need stitches!"

I step back. "I've cut this deep before. It always heals just fine."

"God, Kendra—"

"No doctor!"

"All right, all right. Where's your bandages?"

I point to the clump of grey bandage on the floor with the scab-encrusted pads.

"You don't have anything else?"

"No. I didn't think I was going to cut. It was just going to be a lovely day—with you." *And now I've ruined it all.*

"Okay. Hold on. I'll go get something." She grips my shoulder. "Stay here. You promise?"

"Promise," I whisper. There's no way I'm leaving the bathroom with my arm like this. No way I'm going to let anyone else see it.

"Fine. I'll be right back—five minutes, ten at the most. There's a drugstore around the corner. Just don't move. And hold your arm up. I think that's supposed to help slow down the bleeding."

I feel silly, but I do it anyway.

Meghan reaches for the door handle, then turns back to look at me. "It was from him, wasn't it? The package?"

I nod.

"I'll kill him," she says, and leaves.

27

I lock the door behind her.

"No, you don't want to go in there," I hear Meghan say. "My friend's vomiting. She's got diarrhea, too. Everything. Try the men's bathroom."

I freeze until the voices move away, then grab some clean toilet paper and start wiping the blood off the floor and sink. It smears over the tiles and drips from my arm as I clean. I scrub harder. My stomach feels queasy, like I might really vomit. *I can't believe I did this. Can't believe how out of control I got.*

"You will cut to keep silent—"

I can't believe what I remembered, either. It can't be true. It just can't. Cutting is my *thing. Not his.*

Acid rises up in my throat. *Cutting is what's kept me alive. What helped me when I couldn't take it any more . . . .*

It's what helped me forget.

No! I stagger upright, stare at my wide, frightened eyes in the mirror. *I can't be doing what he wants me to. I can't be!*

There's a knock on the door. I tighten up, watching it like someone's going to burst right through.

"Kendra? It's me," Meghan calls.

I let her in, and she locks the door behind her. Then she puts my arm under the faucet and turns the water on. I flinch as the cold water hits my skin.

"Does that hurt?"

Yes. I shake my head no.

The blood washes from my chaotic slashes, revealing how deep they are before the blood pools up again. Meghan sucks in her breath sharply. She grabs a paper towel and hands it to me. "You'd better dry it. I don't want to hurt you."

I gingerly pat my arm. It's aching fiercely now.

Meghan sits me down on the lid of the toilet seat and starts taking things out of her shopping bag: a roll of gauze bandage, a box of sterile nonstick pads, and some nail scissors. She rips open the packages and gently bandages my arm, wrapping it up tight with the clean, white gauze. I know I should be thanking her, but I just sit there and shiver, feeling sick.

"You okay?" Meghan asks gently—so gently.

"You will cut to forget."

I nod. *I'm so sorry. I never meant for you to see this.* But I don't say it. I can't get my voice to work.

Meghan reaches for my arm, the one that's not hurt, and pulls me up. "Come on. Let's get you out of here."

I nod again and pull my sleeve down over the bandage. I take a step, then another, out of the bathroom.

It's too big a betrayal to be true. He can't have taught

me to cut. I can't just be doing what he wants me to. That would mean I'm letting him win. That would mean I'm still letting him hurt me.

I stumble, and Meghan catches me.

"You okay?" she asks again.

No words. Just shadows fluttering inside me, tearing away my voice. I manage to nod.

She leads me out of the Java Cup, past the staring customers and into the park. We walk back to where we sat earlier and ease down on the grass. Meghan wraps her arms around me and holds me, rocking me gently. A leaf floats down, brushing against my face.

"It's okay. It'll all be okay," she whispers.

But it won't be. How can it?

"Hey! Whatchu starin'at?" Meghan yells over my shoulder, her arm moving sharply against my back. I know she's just given someone the bird.

"Sorry. Look, he got away this time. But he's getting desperate. He'll make a mistake—and then we'll catch him."

I'm the one who made a mistake—by remembering.

No. I shudder. *It was right to remember. I needed to remember. But I need to be able to cut, too.*

"You will cut to forget."

"What's happening, Kendra?" Meghan asks, stroking my sweaty hair.

I clear my tight throat. Move my lips. Form the words. "I think a memory's coming. A big one." *The rest of the memory I don't want to see.*

"You want to call Carolyn?"

"Already did. She's not in." My teeth chatter. "I just want it to go away."

"But it won't, will it? Why don't you just let it come? I'll stay with you."

"I'm afraid to!"

"I know."

Meghan holds me tighter. I shudder as the shadows slice their way through my mind. *His hand closing on my wrist. His breath hot on my cheek. The bathroom door snapping shut behind me—locking.*

I rock against the fear, teeth clenched, trying to hold it all back.

"Let it come, Kendra. Let it come."

Cold floor tiles bite into the bottoms of my feet, making my ankles ache as the cold moves up my legs. The light flickers. The man roughly pushes up my sleeve, chaffing my skin.

"You will learn to keep silent," he says, his voice echoing in the small room.

"No!" I cry, and clutch Meghan's hand.

"I'm right here. Right here with you."

❋

The man pulls a utility knife out of his pocket and pushes the blade up until an inch shows through the handle. The tip of the blade is dull in the light.

"You will cut to keep silent. You will cut to forget. You will cut not to tell. And if you tell, you will cut to kill yourself. You will use your own knife to end your life."

The words are familiar, like I've heard them many

151

times, in many different places. But the voice is the same. His voice. It's always his voice.

"And if you fail, I will kill you myself. I will kill you if you tell."

He grabs my arm, fingers bruising my wrist, and forces the utility knife into my hand. I want to drop it, want to let it go, but his hand closes tightly over mine, crushing my fingers into the handle.

Fear bursts through me, harsh and bright, and I swim up to the top of my head. I shut myself off from my body and mind, shut myself down and go to sleep.

Another part of me steps forward. A part that can follow directions, without reacting. A part that can see the world in shapes and shadows. A part that's a robot.

The man-shape pushes her hand down, fast and hard, making the blade slash into her flesh. The robot is fascinated by the sight of the skin parting open to reveal a bubbly white interior. There is no pain, no feeling. Just parted skin, like an open mouth, and blood rushing up to fill it.

The man-shape hands her a square of white cloth and makes her press it against the wound.

"Now you," he commands.

The robot had watched carefully. The command is clear. Still, her mouth is oddly dry and she feels a strange sensation. But robots don't feel. She knows that.

She brings the blade down to her arm, judging carefully. For some reason, her ears are ringing and her perfectly controlled hand is trembling. She slashes once, twice, at his command.

"If you ever talk about me again, you will slit your own neck. You will do it because you will be sorry that you talked."

He tells her that she can go.

I walk out of the bathroom, not knowing what I am doing there. My arm is screaming with pain. I look down and am terrified. I don't know what's happened, how I got hurt.

I try to remember, but my mind is blank, a thick grey fog filling my head. My mind stretches and twists itself, trying to understand, but nothing makes sense. I start to pull back from the world. And then a voice tells me that I did it to myself, to keep myself from remembering.

I believe the voice. And I remember how to cut.

❁

The shadow lifts slowly. I lie there, exhausted.

Meghan's worried face comes into focus. I can feel her arms around me again, can smell the amber-like honey on her skin. I push myself away.

"It was bad, huh?" she says.

"Oh, yeah."

I shudder; another wave is coming. Meghan holds me tight.

❁

I'm five, maybe six, curled up, naked, shivering, in the bathroom.

The man holds a life-sized plastic arm in front of me,

its surface flesh-colored. He forces the utility knife into my hand.

"This is your arm. Your body," he says. "What will you do if you talk?"

"Cut it," the robot part of me answers automatically, her voice toneless.

"Show me," the man says.

And I do. Over and over, until it becomes a muscle memory, something I can do without thinking. Without looking. Until it's a part of me.

I retch. He was preparing me for it, even then. He was making sure I wouldn't talk.

But I did talk. He didn't manage to stop me. Not completely.

❀

I blink my eyes, forcing myself to focus on the trees, on the grass, on Meghan.

Meghan's watching me, her face tight and pale, and I know this was hard for her. Maybe too hard.

"I'm sorry." I push myself away.

Her hands pull me back. "No. Tell me."

My lips feel cemented together.

"I've been through shit, too, Kendra," Meghan says. "Maybe not as bad as you, but—I can take it. I want to know."

I tell her what I remembered, in slow, halting words.

Meghan rakes her fingers through her hair. "God, he's sick. Just sick."

"I guess."

"You guess? Come on, Kendra, that's pretty scary shit."

"I know, but—" A thought skitters just outside my reach. I grab for it; it's gone.

"But what? And don't tell me it wasn't so bad. I saw your face."

The thought hovers again, darting around my consciousness. I close my eyes, and it comes, chilling my skin.

"Palette knives aren't sharp. They're to spread paint, create texture on the canvas, mix colors. They couldn't cut through cheese. But the one in that package, it had sharp edges like a blade. I took one look at it and cut worse than I ever have before. It was almost like I couldn't stop." I take a shaky breath. "I think that's what he was trying to get me to do. I think he wanted me to kill myself because I've talked about the abuse. Because I've tried to remember who he is. And because I've been using my art to tell."

"Goddamn bastard." Meghan looks like she wants to punch something to keep from crying.

"Hey, it's okay," I say, and it is.

"How can you say that?"

"I know it sounds weird, but I almost feel stronger. Figuring out what he wanted me to do—remembering what he taught me—has made everything clearer. It's like I was painting with only two primary colors before, and now I have the third."

I pull her to me, and we sit there together, listening to each other breathe.

Something blocks out the sun. The stench of alcohol is overpowering. I look up to see a guy leering down at us.

Meghan snaps open her eyes and jerks upright. "Get lost, you pervert."

"You two together?" the man asks, tapping his forefingers together and grinning.

"Just leave us alone, okay?" I say.

"And go screw yourself!" Meghan yells, giving him the bird.

The man holds his hands up mockingly in surrender, then staggers off.

I shiver. "I don't feel like hanging around here any more. You want to go to my place?"

"Yeah. Let's get out of here."

28

When Meghan and I walk in together, Mom sucks in her lips so far they almost disappear. Then she straightens up, puts on her politician smile, and reaches out to shake Meghan's hand. Meghan awkwardly responds.

I don't think I can hold it together much longer; I feel like shit. Taking Meghan's arm, I point her toward the hall. "We're going to my room," I say.

"To do some studying," Meghan adds. Funny girl.

We walk down the hall together, Meghan supporting me without making it look like that's what she's doing, and I close the door behind us.

Meghan looks around slowly. I can see her taking it all in—the organized jumble of paints and brushes, pastels and charcoal on my desk, half covered by rags; the clothes hanging over the back of my chair; the crooked pottery on my windowsill. She doesn't comment on the framed Escher drawings on my walls; the rows and rows of books and CDs on my shelves; my laptop sitting open on the floor; or the tangled sheets on my bed, with my childhood stuffed bunny poking out beneath the covers.

"Sorry about the mess," I say, flinging the sheets over the top of the bunny.

"You kiddin'? This is neat, compared to my room." She keeps looking around, as if my room fascinates her.

My legs start to tremble again, and I sink down onto my bed.

Meghan turns to me, as if she can sense how I'm feeling. "I'm not leaving you alone with this. You don't look so hot."

"I'm all right."

Meghan sits down next to me and puts her hand on my thigh. "No, you're not." She blows out her breath. "Damn it!"

"What?"

"I'm just so angry at what he did to you—at what he's still doing to you—"

"He's not hurting me any more!"

Meghan's eyes fill with tears. "Yes, he is. You know he is. Through what he taught you. And it's driving me crazy to see you hurting this bad. I like you a lot—but I don't know if I'm strong enough for this."

I draw back. "Sarah wasn't."

"I used to see the two of you together all the time. You were so wrapped up in each other, there wasn't room for anyone else."

"She was my first girlfriend."

Meghan waggles her eyebrows up and down. "So the rumors are true."

"I don't know. It depends on what you heard."

Meghan reaches for my hand, strokes my skin. "That

you and Sarah were an item. That someone caught the two of you kissing . . . "

"Right so far."

Meghan hesitates. She lowers her voice. "And then she turned on you, completely flipped out. She told everybody you'd forced her to kiss you, that you'd come on to her."

I close my eyes against the words, then open them again. A few weeks ago, I would have been crying by now. But things have changed. A lot has. "Right again."

"And then she transferred out of school."

"And cut off all contact with me. Refused to answer my calls, texts, or e-mails. Said she'd get a restraining order if I kept harassing her."

"What a bitch!"

I shake my head. "She was just scared. I was, too. I mean, our school's full of homophobia. And she did try to stick it out. Maybe if people hadn't put up posters of us all over the halls or if they hadn't trashed her locker, things might've been different."

"Kendra, you are way too kind to her, after the way she treated you."

I shrug. *I don't know why I'm not more upset. Maybe it's because Meghan is here with me and I know that she likes me. Or maybe it's because I'm so full of pain that I can't feel any more.* "It took me a while, but I think I'm over her. I started being over her the day I met you."

Meghan smiles. "I noticed you the first year of high school. I wanted to get to know you better. Wanted to—" She licks her lips. "Get to know you *much* better. But I figured you weren't a free woman."

She noticed me! My heart flutters.

Meghan's eyes darken. Her hand tightens on mine. "I won't ever do what Sarah did to you; I promise. I don't care what people say."

"I know." I try to smile.

"You're still feeling rotten, aren't you? Because of what that bastard did to you. I can see it in your eyes."

If this was anybody else, I'd be out the door by now. But I'm so drawn to her; I want to be with her, even as I want to run. "I know I'm not good company right now, but would you stay for a while? Would you . . . hold me?"

Meghan wraps her arms around me. I breathe in her scent, relax against her. Her hand moves slowly across my back.

"Are you doing this because you want to?" I ask.

Meghan jerks away from me, her face flushed. "God-damn it! I was trying to comfort you—"

"Because you feel sorry for me?"

"No! Because I think I love you! And I thought I could make you feel better, and then I just wanted to touch you."

I pull her back to me, press her close. This is the first time someone has touched me that I haven't felt *his* hands on me instead. The first time it's actually felt beautiful. Maybe he's finally lost his power over me.

The side door slams. "I'm home!" Dad calls.

Meghan and I jerk apart. For a second, her eyes are wide and startled, and then she grins and says, "When can I see you again?"

I laugh. "Tomorrow," I say.

❀

I miss her already, and it's only been a half hour. I keep reliving our time together, savoring it. I try not to think about the package he sent. Every time I do, I want to cut again. It's crazy.

Dad's heavy footsteps start down the hall toward me. I rush to straighten the covers on my bed. Dad stands in my doorway, looking at me. "You weren't around much, today," he says.

"No...."

"Your mom says you were out with a new friend. And you brought her home afterward."

Don't they have anything to do but talk about me? "Yeah. Meghan."

"Meghan." Dad hesitates, starts jingling the change in his pocket.

I want to laugh. "It's okay, Dad. Yes, I like her, and yes, she's my girlfriend."

Red creeps up Dad's neck and into his cheeks. "Good. That's all we want, your mom and I. We want you to be happy."

"*You* do. I'm not sure Mom does."

"You don't give her enough credit. She loves you, Kendra. She just doesn't want you getting hurt."

"Meghan's not going to hurt me."

"I didn't say she would." Dad sighs and sits down heavily on my bed. "I want to protect you from the world— from heartbreak, from people's prejudices. That's what every parent wants. But I can't always do that. And some things are worth the risk." He looks at me. "Are you happy with this girl?"

"Yes, I think so," I say.

"Then that's what matters." Dad kisses my forehead. "Sleep well, Kendra." He walks back down the hall. I hear him go down the stairs, hear the TV turn on, the canned laughter pouring out. I rub my face. We don't spend much time together any more, not like we used to. I think he misses it.

My cell phone rings—Carolyn's ring tone. I flip open my cell. "Carolyn?" I get up to close my door.

"Kendra! I'm sorry I missed your call. I just heard your message, and you sounded really shaken. How are you doing?"

"Okay. Better now, I think. Way better than when I called you. But it was bad today. Really bad." *The handkerchief falling to the floor. His hand, gripping my wrist.*

"What happened?" she asks. "Do you want to talk about it?" The caring in her voice is so real, I want to tell her everything. But my arm throbs like a warning. "Kendra?" Carolyn says. "You said in your voicemail that he sent you another message?"

"Yeah, he—I—" I see the package again, the white handkerchief and the palette knife against the red tissue paper, like a sea of blood—

The desire to cut comes over me, gripping me fiercely. I close my eyes.

"Kendra? Can you tell me what's going on?"

"No one will ever believe you."

I'm crying suddenly, a deep, panicked sobbing that I can't control. "Hang on," I gasp and dash into the bathroom, locking the door. I turn the faucets on full blast.

"Can you still hear me?" I manage to get out between sobs.

"I hear you. Tell me what happened."

"He—he was trying to silence me again. And it affected me so badly, Carolyn."

"How?"

"I—" But I can't tell her about the cutting. I can't. Panic rips at my chest with sharp claws.

"Kendra?"

I wipe my eyes. "I just—I need to know that you're not going anywhere. That you're going to stick around, no matter what I tell you."

"I promise I'll be here for you as long as you need me," Carolyn says. "Whatever it is, Kendra, I can hear it."

Some of the panic recedes. I take a shaky breath, then another, the sobs fading away. I breathe out slowly, trying to keep myself calm.

I want to tell her so bad, it's a fight to keep the words in. But I just can't tell her about the cutting. His threat, yes. The memory—or parts of it. And Meghan; I can tell her about Meghan. But I can't go into that now. I can't let my parents see me like this. I wipe my cheeks. "I'll tell you Monday, when I see you."

"Are you going to be all right tonight and tomorrow? Until your appointment?"

"Yeah." I shut off the running water. I feel calmer, now. Safer. Even my arm doesn't hurt as much. It helps to know

Carolyn cares. And it helps to know that I won't have to hold on to everything all by myself.

She'll help me sort it out—whatever I tell her.

29

I'm dreaming of Meghan, and I feel so happy. Then her eyes widen, and I follow her gaze to see him *watching us from the shadows.*

His hand grips my shoulder. I'm screaming before I open my eyes, knocking his hand away, still half in the dream. My head is muddled.

"Kendra! It's only me. Wake up, honey," Dad is saying.

I shudder and sit up. *It's Dad. Just Dad.* I struggle to breathe.

"I'm sorry I scared you," Dad says, his voice strained.

"It's okay." I rub my face, trying to collect myself. My arm throbs with pain, and I look down to see rust-colored stains on the sleeve of my nightshirt. I lean back on my arm to hide it, trying to look relaxed. "You wanted something?"

"I wondered if you wanted to go to Sunday school with me this morning. I've been telling the kids about you, about what a good artist you are, and they'd love to meet you."

This again. I grit my teeth. "Not today, Dad." *Why can't I tell him "Not ever"?*

Dad looks closer at me. "You okay, kitten? You look really washed out."

"I'm fine." My arm hurts really badly now, but I can't let him see it.

Dad hesitates. "You sure?"

"I'm sure!" *Just go away.*

Dad straightens up. "All right. Maybe next week."

I wait for a whole minute after he leaves, then I push my sleeve up, unwrap the bandage, and pull off the pads. My arm feels hot under my fingers; the skin around the new wounds is puffy and red. Some of the cuts are oozing yellow pus.

I swallow. I've never seen my arm like this before. I gingerly pull my sleeve back down and stumble to the bathroom.

"You up, Kendra?" Mom calls.

"In a minute!"

I rifle through the medicine cabinet. I don't even know what I'm looking for until I see it—a brown plastic bottle labeled "Hydrogen Peroxide". I have a vague memory of Mom pouring it on my skinned knees when I was little. I uncap the bottle and pour it liberally over my arm; it bubbles and foams up, then disappears down the drain.

"Kendra?" Mom's footsteps click down the hall.

"Coming!" I dash into my room and yank another shirt over the stained one.

Mom comes in. "Your dad thinks you're not feeling well."

"I'm fine." *How many times do I have to say that before they'll leave me alone?*

166

Mom's all dressed up in her best clothes, wearing her makeup, jewelry, and perfume, so she can go to church and pretend that everything's okay.

"Are you coming with us this morning?"

I clench my fists. "Why do you ask me every Sunday? You know I don't go any more."

"It hurts your dad. How do you think it looks, him being a Sunday school teacher and you not even showing up? It's not his fault some man hurt you."

"It's not like I'd go to his class if I went. I'm not a kindergartner any more. Besides, where was God when I was being abused?"

Mom sighs. "I don't have an answer for that—except I'm sure it hurt Him to watch."

He, she, it—if God really exists. I don't want to be having this discussion. "You just want me there so you can look good. I'll bet you haven't told anyone about Dad's job." *Or about the sexual abuse.*

"You're right, Kendra, I haven't. They're not those kinds of friends. And I don't believe in airing our dirty laundry in public."

And you wonder why I don't want to go? I've had too many secrets; I don't need any more. Besides, there's a lot of things I'd rather do. Like be with Meghan.

I clamp down on a smile. "I'm staying home," I say. "See you at lunch."

❀

As soon as they're gone, I phone Meghan. "I've got the house until noon. You want to come over?"

"You kidding? See you in half an hour!"

I shower fast, the hot water stinging my arm. *Meghan's coming!* I find myself singing as I dress. I change my outfit three times before Meghan arrives, checking my armpits for sweat stains and brushing my teeth. My breathing is fast, my head too light—but as soon as I see Meghan, I relax.

"You look so good," she says in a throaty whisper.

I laugh, then reach up to touch her soft hair. "You do, too."

I take her hand and lead her to my bedroom, but as soon as we sit on my bed, we both become awkward and shy.

"How you doin' today?" she asks. "You feeling okay?"

"God, I wish everyone would stop asking me that!"

Meghan pulls back, a hurt look on her face.

I reach for her hand. "I'm sorry! I didn't mean it like that. I'm glad you care. It's just that both my parents asked me the same thing this morning. It made me want to scream. And I feel all muddied inside, trying to see it all— how cutting's helped me and yet that he taught me to do it. They feel like two separate worlds that I can't piece together."

"Maybe you don't want to."

"You're right; I don't. I don't think I can bear it. It's like he's tainted everything important to me, everything I've ever needed—even this."

"He hasn't tainted me," Meghan says, leaning forward.

We kiss—softly at first and then hungrily, almost desperately. I pull back.

Meghan groans.

"Are you sure this is what you want?" I ask.

"Yes, I'm sure." Meghan presses her lips against mine before I can say anything else, and soon I'm lost in our kissing.

Afterward, I look into her flushed face. "I love being with you. But I don't want you to do anything you don't want to. I want there to be only good stuff between us. So any time you want to slow down, just tell me."

Meghan smiles tenderly. "You're so sweet."

I laugh.

"No, really. You are. No one's ever treated me this way before, Kendra. No one's ever asked me how I felt or what I wanted."

I think about the boys she's slept with, and I want to snarl. I glare at the wall.

"What? What just happened?" Meghan asks. Now she's leaning over me.

I'm jealous. That's what. "Nothing!"

"Kendra, one of the things I love about you is that you don't bullshit me. You tell me what's going on. So don't shut me out now."

"All right, all right! I was thinking about all those guys you've…"

"Screwed?"

"Slept with. How probably all they ever cared about was sex. I want you to know that I'll never treat you like that. I'll never use you."

"I know."

"And—maybe I was feeling a little jealous."

"Ha! I knew it!" Meghan play-slaps me. "What kinda girlfriend would you be if you weren't? But Kendra—I'm not going to be with anyone else, not any more, okay? I don't think I could, not now. When we're together, I want to cry and laugh with how good I feel, how connected and happy and alive I am. But when I'm with guys, I'm all shut down. I act like I enjoy it, but I'm waiting to get it over with, waiting to feel something. But I never do. Not like with us."

She touches my hand, and the snarly feeling inside me vanishes.

Meghan glances at her watch. "I should get going, before your folks get home. But I'll see you at school tomorrow."

Meghan strokes my cheek. "We won't be anything like you and Sarah were. I promise."

"I know we won't," I say. And I *do* know. Meghan is strong, right to her core. Strong in a way that Sarah never was.

30

Early morning traffic sounds drift through Carolyn's window. I pick up my mug and take a quick sip of the water she's poured for me. "I don't want to start with the message he sent."

"Okay." Carolyn uncrosses her legs. "What do you want to start with?"

The good news. Then decide how much to tell her. My legs shake. "I think I'm in love."

"Kendra, that's wonderful." Carolyn sets her mug down. "Have you told me about this person before?"

Person. She didn't say "guy." She didn't say "him." I look at her face. She's smiling, leaning forward, her gaze intent on mine.

"It's a girl," I say. "I love another girl."

"Love is love, Kendra. Gender doesn't change that."

"That's not how my parents see it."

"How do they see it?"

"They think that I'm making things harder for myself."

"And do you think that's what you're doing?"

"No! I love Meghan. I feel good with her." I grip my

hands together. "Why aren't you surprised? I mean, that I'm lesbian?"

"You never talk about boys—or about feeling attracted to them," Carolyn says. "But you have talked a lot about other girls. I didn't know for sure; I just kept an open mind." She smiles. "I'm glad you've found someone you like."

"Yeah, me, too." The ferns on her bookshelves seem to nod with me. "I can't remember feeling this happy in a long time. In fact, I don't think I've ever felt this happy. At least, I'm happy when Meghan and I are together. When the memories aren't crashing in."

There it is: The brief sadness in her eyes, the compassion—like she understands what I'm saying on a deep level.

"My mom said you're a survivor. Was she right?"

Carolyn sits back. "Yes, I'm a sexual abuse survivor."

"Why didn't you tell me?" Now *I'm* leaning forward.

"Because it's not my job to burden my clients with my history or my problems. As a therapist, it's my job to help you with yours."

"But it would've helped me to know! I've never met another survivor, never known that anyone could feel really happy again after something so horrible—and you were right here the whole time!"

"I've always told you that happiness was possible for you."

"But being told something is different from seeing it. I can believe it, now that I know about you—now that I've started to feel happy myself. But I didn't believe it was possible before."

Carolyn rubs her chin. "It sounds like I should have

told you. I try to keep my personal life out of my therapy practice as a rule. But I see now that this is one piece of information that might have helped you. I just didn't want to make things strange between us. I'm sorry I didn't tell you."

I love how Carolyn always hears me, even when I'm angry at her; I love how she can admit when she's wrong. I wish, as I always do, that she was my mother. But the pain isn't as strong this time. I know I'll find a way to keep seeing her, find the money to pay for my sessions. And I know that what she gives me is more powerful and less complicated than anything my mother ever could.

"My mom—" I hesitate. "My mom said that she and my dad are going to set up an appointment with you, to try to find out everything I haven't told them."

"Our sessions are confidential; you know that," Carolyn says. "Everything you say here goes no further."

"Even though they're paying you?"

"Even though they're paying me. The only time I would have to break confidentiality is if I thought you were a danger to yourself or to others."

I cross my arms over my chest. "Define *danger*."

Carolyn's eyes become watchful. "Well, if you were seriously thinking of killing yourself, for example. Or of chasing after your abuser with a gun."

"I would never do that!" I laugh.

"Or if you tried to hurt yourself."

"What do you mean, hurt myself? People hurt themselves all the time—smoking when they know it causes cancer, starving themselves to get thin, pushing people away because they're too scared to get close . . . ."

Carolyn nods. "Those are all forms of hurting one-self—especially anorexia. If I suspected you had an eating disorder, I'd have an obligation to tell your parents, since it can be life-threatening. But I was thinking more along the lines of cutting, burning, head banging, that sort of thing."

"Oh, and then you'd have to tell my parents, huh? Therapist-client confidentiality just goes out the window?" I know I should shut up; I know I'm just making things worse, but I can't seem to stop the words from spilling out of me.

Shadows flick through my brain. *"Everyone will betray you,"* his voice whispers. *"Everyone but me."*

"Is there something you want to tell me, Kendra?"

"No, there is not!" I stand up. *Stupid, stupid, stupid.*

"Where are you going?"

"I'm leaving. Getting out of here."

"Our session isn't up."

I walk to the door. "It is now."

31

Carolyn gets up faster than I've ever seen her move before. "Kendra, I know you're upset, I know you're scared—but don't walk away. I want to help you."

"How?" I shout. "By telling my parents? By messing up my whole life?"

"Kendra, how have you hurt yourself?"

This is unraveling too fast. Just two days ago, no one even knew about my cutting. Now too many people know—or suspect. I feel like I'm backed up against a wall, hemmed in on all sides. I tense up, ready to run. "What makes you think I've hurt myself?" I ask.

"By how strongly you reacted," Carolyn says softly. "So what have you done?"

"Why do you want to know?"

"Because I care about you, and I don't want to see you hurting this badly. You don't deserve the anger you're turning on yourself. Your abuser's the one who does."

I look down at my shoes. "That's kind of what Meghan said."

"She was right." Carolyn takes a step toward me and

holds out her hand—the same one she's placed on my shoulder when I'm going through memories, to help bring me back; the hand that's held mine and helped me feel safe. "Why don't you show me what you've done?"

"Who says I've done anything?"

"I think you've told me in a hundred different ways today. I'm so sorry I didn't pick up on it sooner."

"This is not your fault! It's not anyone's fault!" I'm crying now. "No one gets it. Cutting *helps* me! It really does!"

"Cutting," Carolyn says softly. She takes a step closer, and I let her. "How does it help you?"

"It takes away the pain when I can't stand it any more. It helps me breathe. Helps me think." I glance at Carolyn. She's not freaking out, just looking sad. I rub my arm. "It stops the memories when nothing else will. And they've been bad lately. Really bad. I almost saw his face, Carolyn. And I can't let that happen. He'll kill me if I do."

"Oh, honey." Carolyn closes the distance between us and puts her arms around me, and I let her.

I feel so safe in her arms, like nothing can hurt me.

"He won't kill you. That's something he told you to keep you quiet. It's a common threat that pedophiles use."

"I don't think he's a regular pedophile," I say, looking up at her. "He wrote that note. And then he sent an MP3 telling me to keep silent—but his voice was wonky, digitized like a computer's. And then he sent me a package."

Carolyn's arms tighten around me.

"And he's been following me again."

"He's really trying to intimidate you."

"Yeah, well, it's working!"

"I know it's frightening," Carolyn says. "That's what he wants. He wants to scare you so much that you'll never reveal his name."

"There's something else," I say. I pull away. "He's the one who taught me to cut."

"He *taught* you?"

I tell her fast, the words jumbling over each other. "But I've been thinking about it. There's no way of knowing whether I'd have turned to cutting on my own if he hadn't taught me to. I could have; it does help me cope. So maybe I'm not just doing what he wants me to. Maybe I'm doing what I need to do."

"It's frightening to think he had that much control over you, isn't it?"

"Yes." I shudder.

"And as you said, there's no way to know. It sounds like it's very painful for you to even consider. But I think his teaching you must have predisposed you to cutting."

I bite my lip. "I don't want to talk about it."

"All right. We'll leave it for now. But will you let me see where you cut?"

"Why?" I take a step back.

"Because I care. And I'm concerned. I want to see it for myself."

"All right, all right." This is becoming a whole routine. I turn away, roll up my sleeve and unwind the gauze. I hesitate a moment, then tear the pads off. Then I turn back around so she can see.

Carolyn draws in her breath sharply. "Those should have had stitches."

"Why?" I look at them. "It's not like I was going to bleed to death."

"Because you cut so deep, Kendra. And you *are* playing with death. Every time you cut yourself, every time you bleed, you're cutting through a vein."

"I've been cutting for six months, now—*six months*—and it's been okay!"

"Six months?" Carolyn blows out her breath. "That's a long time. I wish I'd known sooner. But Kendra—you *are* taking a chance. Cut through an artery or a major vein, and you could bleed to death before you could even call for help."

I clench my fists. *I don't care! Nothing else makes the pain go away. Nothing else stops the shadows.*

"You don't want to hear that, do you?"

"No!" *Because I need cutting. I need it so bad.* I can't look at her.

"I know you probably can't stop just like that." Carolyn snaps her fingers. "And I'm not asking you to; it's been helping you cope."

I look into her kind, worried eyes. She's on my side; I know she is.

"I just want you to try to do other things instead, if you can. Your body's been through so much abuse; it doesn't deserve to be punished more. *You* don't deserve this abuse, this repeated threat to your life."

I nod slowly. I don't want to die. But I don't know how to give up cutting, either.

"What did you use to do this?"

"A utility knife. Well, the blade from one."

"Can I see it?"

"How did you know I had it on me?"

"I didn't know for sure, but I suspected. Come on, Kendra. What can it hurt?"

I bend down and dig the blade out of my sock, then give it to her, my hand shaking. If she tries to take it away, I'll just buy another one or I'll find something else, anything that will cut with precision. I'm not going to stop cutting. I can't.

"Do you wash this before you use it?"

"No."

Carolyn hands the blade back to me.

I tuck it back into my sock, trying not to feel so exposed, trying not to feel the shame that's heating my face.

"I want you to wash the blade with soap and water beforehand. Wash your arm, too, if you think you're going to cut—if you absolutely can't avoid it." She goes back to looking at my arm, gently turning it over. Her fingers are cool and reassuring against my hot skin. "These look infected. Did you put anything on them?"

"I poured some hydrogen peroxide on it yesterday."

"Hydrogen peroxide is good." Carolyn walks over to her bookshelf and pulls out a first aid kit, then brings it back to the couch. She sits down and motions for me to sit beside her. I do.

Carolyn takes out a tube and unscrews the cap. "You can also put anti-bacterial ointment on your wounds; it'll prevent infection." She globs some on my arm, spreading it lightly and holding her breath like she doesn't want to hurt me. "I want you to put some of this on every day, all right?"

"Okay." Somehow, I don't mind her telling me what to do. Part of me even likes it. It feels like something a good mom might do.

Carolyn screws the cap back on the tube and hands it to me. "I'm taking this seriously, Kendra, because it is serious. I want you safe. I want you to stay alive. And I don't want to see you hurt any more. You've been hurt too much already."

I stare down at my hands. She sounds so worried—so unhappy. I *need* the cutting—need it to get me through the pain. But some of the comfort's gone, now that I feel her worry for me—and her fear.

"We're going to work on some things you can do instead of hurting yourself—distraction, self-soothing, expressing your feelings. And if memories come flooding in on you, I want you to tell me, okay? We need to help you close them down when you're not here in session with me so you don't feel such a need to cut."

I nod.

Carolyn pats my knee. "I'm so glad you told me. Just remember that you can call me any time. We can talk things through. I'd rather you do that than cut." Carolyn picks up one of her business cards, and writes on it. "This is my cell. I don't give it to everyone. But I want you to use it if you think you're going to cut."

"Are you mad at me?"

"No, of course not. I'm a little sad that you felt you needed to do this. And I'm sad that I didn't see it sooner. But I'm glad you trusted me enough to tell me now."

"Are you going to have to tell my parents?"

"You know I will."

I rub my hands on my jeans. "When—?"

"As soon as you leave."

"But you won't tell them anything else, right?" I say. "You won't tell them about my memories or the MP3 player or anything else?"

"Absolutely not. The only thing I'll share with them is your self-harm. I'm legally and morally bound to tell them about it. But I promise, I will not share anything else."

I pinch the inside of my hand, trying not to cry.

"It'll be all right, Kendra. It'll work itself out."

But I don't know how it can.

32

I pass people on the way to school, but I don't really see them. I don't see anything except Carolyn's worried face. Right now, she's probably dialing my parents' number, telling them my secret.

I want to run back to her office and snatch the phone from her, beg her not to call. But I know I can't do that, so I just keep walking.

Everything is getting so messed up. I wish I could start the morning over, but it's too late to change it now. At least I'll see Meghan soon. And Mrs. Archer, too. I need to see their friendly faces, need to know they care.

I run my fingers along the rough brick of a building, letting it scrape my skin, drawing blood. The stinging pain only irritates me; it doesn't soothe me the way cutting does. I don't know why everyone thinks cutting is such a big deal. It's not like I'm running around hurting anyone else.

An empty ginger ale can lies in the gutter. I know that if I have to, I can tear it apart and use it to cut . . . .

"Kendra!" A car pulls up beside me.

I freeze, my heart clenching. Why didn't I stay alert to my surroundings? I shake myself and start to run.

182

"Kendra!" I swear I hear Mom's voice.

I stop and turn around. Mom's leaning out the car window, her cheeks wet with tears. Dad's sitting stiffly beside her at the wheel. I walk slowly to the car.

Dad leans across Mom to look at me. "Get in the car, Kendra," he says in a jagged voice.

"Why? What's happening?"

"We're going to Carolyn's, all three of us."

❀

It's quiet in the car—too quiet. I can hear every sniffle Mom makes, every grunt of Dad's breath. I can't believe this is happening so fast, can't believe we're heading right back to Carolyn's.

I know from the way Mom's trying not to cry and the way Dad's avoiding my gaze that they know about the cutting. I feel hot with shame and dirty somehow, like I've done something wrong. And I have. I've hurt them.

My head gets light. I float up and out of myself and look down at our car, on all three of us, sitting in silence. It's so familiar, this drifting outside of myself. I know I've done it before; I've done it often.

I follow my parents into the building, all of us locked in our own tomb-like hush. The silence pushes up beneath my skin and I scream inside—but nothing comes out. Fear grows like ice inside me, splintering into my heart.

Carolyn opens her door; her gaze finds mine, and I feel myself come back to my body just a little. A tiny spot of warmth spreads through my ice-cold stomach.

Dad sits at one end of the couch; Mom sits at the other, taking my regular spot. I want to tip the couch over, to shove them right out of the office. They don't belong here, with their heavy sighs and stilted voices. They're invading this space that used to be mine—mine and Carolyn's.

Dad pats the cushion beside him, and I sit where they expect me to—imprisoned by Mom on one side and Dad on the other. I draw myself in tight, but Dad's knee still bumps into mine and Mom squeezes my hand.

"I don't understand why this has happened," Mom says, looking at Carolyn.

I roll my eyes. *Isn't it obvious?*

Dad draws himself upright. "What I want to know is how long you've known that Kendra was cutting herself. Did you know from the beginning?"

"No," Carolyn says, "I just found out today. That's why I called you."

"And we appreciate that. But I guess you'll understand when we tell you that we're taking her elsewhere."

I jerk back like he's slapped me. "That's not fair! It's not Carolyn's fault. I kept it a secret from everyone. She's the one who got me to talk."

"It's too little, too late, Kendra. I know it'll be hard to adjust to someone new, but I want what's best for you. And right now, Carolyn isn't it."

There's something wrong with his voice, something wrong with his words. But I can't figure out what, can't hold the thoughts still in my head.

"I understand this is hard for you, Mr. Marshall," Carolyn says. "It must've been quite a shock. But I don't think changing therapists right now will help Kendra."

"Don't talk to me like I'm one of your clients," Dad snaps. "Just tell me why I should continue to pay you to see my daughter, when she was cutting herself to pieces right under your nose."

Mom lets out a muffled sob.

I want to cry out with her. I never meant to hurt her. I never meant to hurt anyone at all. And now I've hurt so many people. I bite down hard on my lip. If only I hadn't told Carolyn . . . . If only I hadn't let her see.

"Kendra wasn't harming herself in our sessions," Carolyn says slowly. "And there *is* control in the act." She hands a box of tissues to my mom. "I don't think it's helpful for us to keep going over what has or hasn't been done; I think what we need to look at right now is how we can support Kendra."

"That's my priority, too," Dad says. "I just don't think this therapy is working for her. Look at what she's been doing!"

"I can understand your concern," Carolyn leans forward. "But her behavior is not an indication that she's getting worse. It's merely a symptom of her distress."

"I'm sorry," Mom says, crumpling the tissues in her fist. "I don't understand."

"Self-injury shows the depth of pain and turmoil someone is feeling. Now, I know you'll want her to stop hurting herself right away. But a more realistic hope is that Kendra will learn some new coping skills, and, in time, find the tools and strategies she needs to safely express her emotions instead of cutting. I feel certain that Kendra can do this. She's very strong."

But I don't feel like I am.

"She *is* strong," Dad says, his voice choking up. "We know that. But she's been through so much; I want to make sure that we're doing the right thing. That we're not harming her more."

"Therapy *helps* me, Dad."

He turns to me. "I'm not convinced. Don't you think it's odd that you didn't cut until you entered therapy? Doesn't that worry you?"

"Therapy doesn't have anything to do with my cutting! Therapy's what's kept me alive. And Carolyn."

"What are you saying, Kendra?" Dad asks, his face tightening into a frightened mask. "You've been thinking about suicide?"

Mom gasps beside me.

I don't know how we got here. I never meant to tell them any of this. I can hear Mom's labored breathing, and feel the tension in Dad. I shift on the sofa and pull myself further inward. "Yes, I was thinking about it—*before* therapy. But that's what I'm saying. Carolyn's helped me want to live, and I'm past that now. And isn't it better that I cut myself than kill myself?"

"Oh, my God," Mom says.

Dad pinches the bridge of his nose. "You were thinking about killing yourself," he says softly.

I look at Carolyn, silently begging her to help me.

"Kendra has gone through a very rough period," Carolyn says in her soothing voice. "Many survivors do, when they first remember their abuse. But Kendra is a strong, resilient girl, and she's making remarkable progress. I would say that suicide is the farthest thing from her mind right now. She's told me quite clearly that she wants to live."

I nod my head hard.

"Self-harm is not an act of failed suicide," Carolyn says, leaning forward. "It's the act of trying to cope with unbearable pain. It can also be a cry for help—a cry I'm taking very seriously. Kendra needs our support. And I intend to be here for her."

"And make a buck off her," Dad says.

I can't believe he said that. "Carolyn cares about me!" I glare at him. "You're just worried about the money because you can't afford it."

"Hush, Kendra; that's private family business," Mom says.

"It doesn't matter. I'll pay for my own sessions."

"Money *is not* the issue," Dad says. "How do we know that this woman has your best interests at heart?"

"Mr. Marshall," Carolyn says, "I know you're upset, but—"

"All I'm saying is that she wasn't cutting before she came to see you." Dad jiggles his foot, his pant leg rising above his sock to reveal dark, curly hair that glitters against the paleness of his skin.

He reaches down to scratch his leg. The sound of his nails on his dry flesh is loud, and shivers shoot up my spine.

And then all I can see is his hand—the way the dark hair sprouts from each finger, the blunt way his nails are cut. I see it—*and I recognize it.*

I recognize *his* hand, his face, his voice. The fragments of memory all slam together in a burst of blinding pain.

33

I press my hands to my aching head. Their voices move in and out around me, their words devoid of meaning.

It can't be Dad. It can't be!

But I know it is. I know it with my whole being. I know, now, why I was afraid to remember, why I thought I couldn't survive it. My abuser lives with me. He lives right in the same house.

Shadows rip through my brain, pounding behind my eyes: *Dad's face looming over me. His hand gripping my wrist. His lips against my ear. I feel his fingers bruise my skin and the familiar pressure of his body against mine; I hear his voice, the voice I know so well, that deep voice I've been trying so hard to ignore.*

His sweat smell fills my nostrils—sweat and sex and blood—and I think I'm going to vomit. Bright spots shimmer before me.

Their voices are still rising and falling in waves, but I can't hold onto them, can't separate them into words. I want to smash my head against the wall, to empty it of the memories. But I know they're not going away, not ever again.

Carolyn leans forward and touches my knee. It's a quick, fast movement. But it's enough to remind me that she's with me—and that she cares. I breathe in and feel the floor beneath my feet again, see Carolyn's kind face, and smell her peppermint tea.

Sound comes back. Voices, too.

"I don't think you understand how important this is," Dad is saying, his body stiff and hard.

I inch away from him, pushing myself into Mom.

"Kendra doesn't tell us anything, just like she didn't tell you about the cutting. If you can just tell us who abused her, maybe we can see that justice is done. At the very least, we can keep her safe from the bastard."

Carolyn crosses her legs. "I understand your concern. But even if Kendra had told me this man's identity, I couldn't reveal it without her permission. You know, Mr. Marshall, opening up repressed memories is a long, slow process. It takes a lot of time and patience."

Dad relaxes beside me. Silently, I thank Carolyn. She said the right thing without even knowing it.

"Then I don't think we have any further business here," Dad says. He gets up, reaching out to shake Carolyn's hand. "Nice putting a face to your name."

Carolyn slowly stands to meet him. "Likewise."

Mom gets to her feet. "Thank you for seeing us today."

"Of course." Carolyn turns to me and opens her arms for a hug. I cling to her, wanting her to save me, wishing I could tell her without saying it aloud.

"Kendra, are you coming?" Dad asks from the doorway.

I pull away. "I just want to say good-bye. Give me a minute, okay?"

His face is like a mask, his eyes hard and searching. I push the fear and knowledge down as hard and as far as I can, and try to look at him the way I'd look at Sandy, without fear or revulsion.

"All right." Dad takes his keys out of his pocket. "We'll start down the hall without you—but I expect you to catch up. We have a lot of talking to do."

He turns and leaves. Mom follows close behind him.

I wait for their footsteps to fade, then I turn to Carolyn. "It's him," I whisper. "He's the one! It's my dad."

Her face pinches tight and I know she understands.

Then I turn and run.

34

We're all silent in the car, like the shock has stolen our voices. Rain spatters the windshield, drumming on the hood. The rhythmic thunk of the windshield wipers makes the silence seem even more oppressive. Dad drives without looking at either of us.

I pinch at the soft web of skin between my thumb and index finger, trying to stay calm. I don't know how I'm going to act normal when we get home. I'm not sure I can be in the same house with him. Not sure I can sit in this car much longer.

Mom turns around in her seat to face me. "I got a strange phone call today, Kendra. From some woman at the Java Cup."

"Can this wait, Mom? Because I really don't think—"

"She wouldn't tell me anything when I said you weren't in. She wouldn't even leave a message. So I went down there to talk to her, to find out what she wanted with my daughter. And you'll never guess what I saw."

I cover my face with my hands. "Mom—"

"Your art was on display! Twenty pieces—none of

191

which I'd seen before. *None* of them! I looked like a fool, with everyone congratulating me when I hadn't known a thing about it!" Mom takes a shuddering breath. "Why did you keep it a secret from me? Didn't you think I'd want to know? Didn't you think I'd care?"

I take my hands away from my face. Mom's glaring at me with angry eyes, but her mouth's quivering. It reminds me of how sometimes when I'm trying not to cry, I lash out instead, hoping no one will see my pain.

Mom insecure…because of me?

"You always criticize my art," I say. "It's never good enough for you."

"You told me you'd stopped painting."

"No. I just stopped showing you what I paint."

"All I've ever done is try to help you paint pictures that people would want to buy."

"But they *do* want to buy my paintings, Mom." *At least one person does.*

"What's in these paintings?" Dad asks, gripping the wheel so tight his knuckles look like they're going to split through his skin.

I answer fast, before Mom can. "They're just fantasy— a girl flying, a woman turning into a tree . . . . "

Dad's grip relaxes.

Mom opens her mouth to speak.

I lean forward. "I was going to tell you, but I wanted to make sure people liked them first."

"Your father didn't know, either?"

"No, I did not." Dad clenches the steering wheel again, a muscle twitching in his cheek.

Good one, Mom.

"I wonder what other secrets she's keeping from us." He turns around to glare at me in the backseat. "What are you hiding, huh? What else has slipped your mind?"

"Henry! The road—watch the road!" Mom screams, grabbing his arm.

Dad swings back around. "Shit!" The car swerves across the slick road. Dad jerks it back into our lane as horns blare at us from two lanes of traffic.

"Well, Kendra?" Dad looks at me in the rearview mirror, waiting for me to answer.

"There's nothing to tell you. I'm not hiding anything."

"But you have," Dad says. "First you kept the cutting from us, then you kept this art show a secret. I'm not sure we can trust you any more."

"Henry, I wouldn't go that far," Mom says.

"Well, I would! Look at her sitting there with that smug look on her face!"

My heart flutters. "It's not like that."

"It's not, is it?" Dad hits the steering wheel. "I think you've been playing me for a chump. I'll bet you know exactly who raped you, don't you?"

This can't be happening. "I told you, Dad. I don't know who did it!" I shout. "I can't remember his face."

Dad snorts. "You've been drawing this whole thing out—just so you could keep seeing that woman, the one who's been putting crazy ideas into your head! It's her you're in love with!"

What? In love with Carolyn? I stare at the back of his head. *He can't really think that, can he?* "You've got it all wrong."

Mom keeps turning back and forth between us, like she doesn't quite understand what's happening.

Get a clue, Mom. "Carolyn's been *helping* me," I say. "She's my *therapist! I* am *so* not in love with her."

"You think Kendra's in love with her therapist?" Mom says. "Honey, that's not it at all. Don't you remember? It's this girl she likes, this girl her own age. If anything, Carolyn's like a mother to her."

They're both jealous of Carolyn. I chew my lip. *I'm in such deep shit. I have to figure out how to convince Dad I don't know what he did. Either that, or run.*

I reach for my door handle; it's locked. They're all locked; Dad's got the master controls. He meets my gaze in the mirror.

I pinch my hand harder. "I don't know who abused me. Believe me, if I did, you'd be the first to know." *I have to talk my way out of this. Have to make him believe me.* "I wish I could remember, because someone's been stalking me. And it's got to be him."

"What?" Mom swivels around, her eyes bulging. "You never told me that!"

"I was afraid." I shrug. "But I'm telling you now. If only I could remember his face, I'd feel safer. I mean, we could stop him then, right?"

"Of course we could," Mom says. "I can't believe you didn't tell us! Someone's been stalking you, and you didn't think we'd want to know?"

Her shrill voice demands my attention, but I'm looking at Dad. I see that his fingers haven't relaxed their death grip on the steering wheel, that his back is stiff, and that a muscle's twitching in his jaw. I'm scared—so scared that my thoughts slow down as if that'll slow down what's happening.

"Did you hear that, Henry?" Mom says. "That bastard's been stalking her."

Dad grunts.

We turn the corner and start up our street. I clutch the backs of their seats. The seat belt bites into me. "Can't we just—uh—can't we stop off at the Java Cup so I can show you my paintings?" I hardly know what I'm saying. I just know I have to distract him. "I feel bad that you never saw them."

But Dad doesn't answer; he just drives faster.

"Henry, slow down," Mom says. "What's gotten into you?"

The wheels screech as Dad turns into our driveway. He shuts off the engine, but he doesn't move.

Mom reaches for the door handle, clicking it back and forth. "Henry. Henry? Open the doors!"

Dad just sits there, his head bowed, his shoulders hunched; but there is a coiled, spring-like quality to his body, a held-in tightness that scares me.

Mom touches his arm tentatively. "Henry, what's wrong? You're not still upset about Kendra blurting out our financial problems, are you? It doesn't matter if that woman knows; she's not part of our circle."

Dad lifts his head. "You're right. It doesn't matter." His eyes are cold as slabs of marble. "The only ones that matter are you, me, and Kendra. We're just one big happy family. Isn't that right, Kendra?"

"That's right," I say, swallowing.

Dad unlocks the doors.

35

I swing open my door, but Dad's already out of the car, blocking my way. He grabs my arm.

"I want to talk to you," he says. He leans toward me, lowering his voice. "Don't try to run, or I won't be held responsible for what I do."

My thoughts skitter away. I'm on autopilot—just a shell of a body, following his commands.

Dad steers me toward the side of the house, and I walk with him, cold rain bouncing off my forehead and my cheeks and sliding down my collar. He waits until Mom unlocks the door, then shoves me inside, ahead of him.

The dim entrance smells like old sweat. I edge over to the stairs, moving out of Dad's reach. The maps on the walls seem to mock me from a time when I thought our house was safe—when I thought I was safe with Dad.

Mom's looking at us like she doesn't understand what's happening. But we've been here before, Mom, Dad, and me. Mom turning away when I tried to tell her, pretending she didn't understand. Dad threatening me, trying to keep me silent. And me, afraid to even speak.

We're each in the same roles again, only the stakes are higher now. I'm not a child any more; I can't be bullied the same way. And this time, it's my sanity, my life that I'm fighting for. I can't let him win. But he can't afford to let me win, either.

Dad's standing in the doorway, blocking the exit like a human barricade. He watches me silently, waiting for me to make a move. There's no way I could get past him. If I try to outrun him to the front door, he's taller than me—and still faster.

I chew my lip, ripping off a piece of skin. Will he try to stop me if Mom goes with me? I grip her arm. "Mom! Let's go. Let's get out of here, right now!"

Mom's face is blank. "Why, honey?"

No one can be this out of it. "Dad's the one who raped me."

"Don't you tell lies," Dad says, his voice low and controlled. "You know all I ever did was love you." He reaches for me.

I back away. "Mom! Come on!"

"You're not leaving this house, either of you," Dad says. "Not until we work this out."

"What do you mean?" Mom says. "I know you're upset, Henry, but—"

"Upset?" Dad growls. "You have no idea."

I stare at Mom, my body growing heavy and still. "Mom, didn't you hear me?"

Mom narrows her eyes. "I heard you, Kendra. I heard you, but I don't believe you. How can you stand there and say things like that? How can you think up something that sick?"

"I'm not making it up! He raped me, Mom! Every night, while you were sipping tea and eating biscuits, he raped me."

"No. I would have known!" Mom covers her mouth with her shaking hand. "You're just making it up because you're jealous that he loves me best. You always wanted to be his favorite. But I'm the one he wants!"

I hear the desperation in her voice, hear how she's trying to convince herself, even now. And I know she won't help me—again.

"Kendra, think carefully," Dad says. "Do you really want to tear apart our family like this?"

I'm not the one who tore it apart.

I take a step back. Despair fills me like wet earth, heavy and suffocating. I can barely keep my head up. I look at Mom. "Do you know that every night, I prayed that this would be it, Mom? That this would be the night you'd finally save me?"

"I'm sorry, Kendra, but I can't let you do this," Dad says. His hands close around my neck, squeezing hard.

He's choking off my air, just like he did before, all those years ago. My throat aches. I don't know if Mom saved me then or if she'll save me now. I only know that I have to fight.

I strike out with my knees, my feet, and both my fists. It's instinctive; I must breathe. I don't want to die. But Dad's strong, so much stronger than me. Darkness begins edging into my sight; my lungs burn.

I can hear my own wheezing below Mom's screams.

The pain is tight and sharp in my chest. And then my knee connects with his crotch. His hands fall from my throat.

Air floods back in, burning my throat and lungs. I'm gasping, almost gagging on air.

Dad's doubled over, clutching himself. And Mom's just standing there—still screaming. *Thanks, Mom.*

I run for the front door, skidding along the polished wood of the halls, then the worn, bare carpet of the living room. Paintings knock against the walls as I run.

Mom sounds like a shrieking kettle, going on and on. I jerk at our heavy front door. Locked!

I fumble with the bolt, my sweaty fingers slipping, and finally it turns. I yank the door open. But as the light from outside pierces my eyes, I hear a click from behind me.

Then I hear his voice: "Walk out that door, and you're dead."

36

I stand there, my heart pounding like it wants to rip right out of my chest.

Mom's screeched words start to reach me. "Put down that gun!"

Gun?

I turn around, the world in slow motion.

Dad's standing there, pointing a handgun at my chest. "Don't even think about it," he says.

In four steps, he's beside me, slamming the door shut. He locks it again, then motions with his gun toward the living room, where Mom is standing.

"Henry! What do you think you're doing?" Mom screams.

I wish she'd stop screaming, give me time to think.

"I'm trying to bring us to an understanding," Dad says. "So shut up, Lori, before I shut you up."

Mom shuts up abruptly.

"Good." Dad smiles grimly, his eyes like a stranger's. "Now sit. Both of you."

Mom and I sit together on our faded couch. I clutch

the edge of the seat cushion, the rough material scratching my hands.

My cell phone rings loudly, playing Carolyn's ringtone. I slide my cell out of my pocket, wishing I'd had it on vibrate.

"Give it to me," Dad says, holding out his hand.

If I let him take it, I'm giving up my last link to safety.

"Give it to me, now!" Dad screams, waving the gun at me, the chords in his neck bulging.

I stumble over and hand it to him.

He rips out the battery, then stomps on the phone, shattering it. "That's better," he says, sounding pleased. "Now, go sit back down."

I scramble to the couch.

"What are you going to do to us?" Mom asks in a quavering voice.

"Why would I do anything to you? This is all one big misunderstanding. Isn't that right?"

Mom gulps and turns her head away.

Dad's soldiers, the ones he made from model kits, are lined up on the mantle beside me, like a miniature firing squad. For some reason, I have this crazy desire to laugh.

Then the phone rings shrilly in the kitchen.

"I should get that," Mom says, rising.

Dad waves the gun at her. "Sit down!"

She sits.

The phone stops ringing, and then starts again. Probably Carolyn. Or Meghan, wondering why I'm not in class. I lick my dry, chapped lips.

I've already given up my bargaining chip: pretending

I don't remember him. I wasted it on Mom, thinking she'd protect me. But she's never protected me—not when it mattered.

The ringing stops, and the room goes so quiet, I can hear Mom's breathing beside me.

"Let us go, Dad. Put the gun away, and everything can go back to normal."

The phone rings again, insistently.

Dad spins around and shoots it, once, then twice. The ringing stops.

Dad turns back to glare at me, his eyes dark. "You think I'm stupid?"

"Of course not. I swear I haven't told anyone. No one except you—and Mom just now. And she'll forgive and forget like she always does—won't you, Mom?"

Mom looks at me with big, wide eyes.

"Won't you?" I say again. I want to poke her, to make her speak.

Mom nods.

Dad wipes his sweaty forehead with his handkerchief. It's white, like the one in the package he sent me.

"You told that scheming therapist, didn't you? I knew she was no good for us. You started changing, looking at me differently, as soon as you started seeing her."

"No, Dad, I didn't! I swear I didn't! I didn't even know it was you—" *Please, God, let him believe me.* "Until the drive home today. The way you were acting, I knew there was something wrong, and then I figured it out. I haven't told anyone. I haven't had time."

"I don't know whether I can trust you."

"You can trust me, Dad."

"But why, Henry? I don't understand why," Mom wails beside me.

I grit my teeth. I want to hit her, to make her shut up before she sets Dad off again.

Dad sinks down onto a chair across from us, the springs groaning under his weight. He looks like he's going to cry.

"I thought if I got married, it would change everything. You looked so young, Lori, with your smooth skin, just like a child's, and I thought it would be enough. I prayed that it would be. But then we had Kendra—" He makes a moaning sound. "And I couldn't help myself."

I'm going to be sick, right here on our khaki-green carpet. I clench my teeth as my stomach lurches, and I force the acid back down.

His face is full of pain, like he really doesn't like what he's done. But I can't allow my heart to twist itself up for him. Not if I want to get out of here alive.

"Dad—"

"Kendra, I tried. I really tried to stop," Dad says. "But I couldn't. It's like an addiction, but a hundred times worse. I can't control it." He moans again. "Can you ever forgive me?"

I grit my teeth. I can't listen any more. Because if I do, I'm going to start screaming and never stop. I stare at the heavy green drapes pulled across the front window. If only Mom would say something intelligent; if only she'd try to calm him down. But I can't ever depend on her for help. I take a shaky breath. "I forgive you, Dad. I mean, you stopped, didn't you?"

"You bet I did," Dad says. "I stopped when you were twelve. You were beginning to develop, and you didn't look like a child any more. And you were starting to fight me. I couldn't control you as easily."

When I was twelve. That was only three years ago. My stomach cramps so hard, I almost double over. It was three years ago that Dad started teaching Sunday school—to five-year-olds. Five-year-olds in a closed classroom, while all the adults are upstairs, praying.

My body turns cold, then hot. Why didn't I guess? Why didn't I ever see it? Guilt washes through me in a wave so strong I can hardly keep from crying out. I wonder if this is how Mom feels about me. Is this why she couldn't bear to see what was happening?

A thought sears through my mind, and I frown at the carpet. *If Dad stopped raping me three years ago, why did he only want me to cut just six months ago?*

My teeth start to chatter. I grit them together. *Because that's when I started remembering. That's when I started being a danger to him. I started being someone who could keep him away from other children—from his new victims.*

Dad fingers his gun, tracing its edges, and I know he's thinking about death. Maybe about mine. Or Mom's.

I have to talk him out of this. My throat is so tight, I can barely speak. "Let us go, and I swear I won't tell. No one'll ever know."

Mom shudders beside me.

Dad jumps up, pointing the gun at me again. "How stupid do you think I am?" he roars.

"I don't think you're stupid. I'm offering my silence in exchange for our lives."

Dad's face crumples, tears rolling down his darkened cheeks. The gun droops in his hand. "I never wanted this. I'm not a monster, Kendra. Really. I'm not. I'm just a man who needs things."

But I won't let his words in, not any more. I won't believe his lies.

I stand up and hold out my hand. "I'll help you. And Carolyn will. Just give me the gun, Dad. Just give me the gun."

"No!" Dad's arm shakes as he points the gun at me again. "I'm not going to let you trick me."

"I'm trying to help you," I say. "Please let me help you. And let Carolyn help. She'll know what to do—"

The gun wobbles in his hand. "Shut up!" he yells, squeezing the trigger.

37

The bullet slams past me, penetrating the living room wall. Mom's face is white; her lips are moving like she's praying, but she isn't making any sound.

My legs tremble so hard, I'm not sure I can keep standing. But I can't sit down again; I've got to get the gun.

"Dad," I say, taking a step forward.

He steadies the gun, pointing it at me. "Don't move, Kendra. I'm warning you. I don't want to hurt you—but I'm not going to jail. I'm not going to lose everything I have."

Suddenly there's pounding on the door. "Police! Open up!"

Dad swivels around to face the door, then whirls back. He jabs his finger toward me. "Now look what you've done. This is all your fault. You did this!"

"No, I didn't. How could I?"

"You called them here."

"When would I have called them?" I say. "I've been with you the whole time."

Dad shakes his head and clenches the gun tighter.

"When you asked to be alone with that therapist, that's when!"

"No, Dad. I swear, I didn't." *But Carolyn might have.*

"Police! Open up, now!" The shout comes again, followed by the pounding on the door.

Dad closes the distance between us. Then he hooks his arm around my neck and drags me to the door, the cool barrel of the gun pressed against my temple. It smells of oil and burnt gunpowder, and I choke on the smell.

I don't want to die!

Dad drags me sideways to the front window and shoves back the curtains, keeping me in front of him. "Get away from the house!" he shouts to the police, his voice wild. "Get away, or I'll shoot her. I'll kill her in front of you all!"

His words rip through me like shrapnel. *He means it! He's willing to kill me to save himself.*

"Well? What's it going to be?" Dad shouts.

An officer's eyes meet mine. Another officer winces. I watch them raise their hands, palms up, and slowly back away. Then I hear the heavy clunk of their boots on our porch as they back away. They're leaving!

I want to scream at them not to leave me here, but I can't seem to make my voice work; I can't shout anything at all.

Behind the cops, I see red and blue lights flashing, pulsing out a signal of distress, and a TV crew pointing a camera at our house. A small crowd of people shove each other, straining to look past the police barricade. I don't know how they can watch and not do something. *Why are they even here?* My blood roars in my ears, and my legs begin to sag.

"Damn reporters, listening in on the police scanners," Dad says, jabbing at me with the gun. "You see what you did? You see what you got us into?"

He yanks me back from the window, his arm still tight around my neck, and I pray that I survive—that Mom and I both get out of here alive.

38

A phone rings faintly, somewhere in the house. The sound jars us all.

"Goddamn phones," Dad says, his arm pressing hard against my windpipe. "Why won't they leave us alone?"

Choking, I pull at his arm; he loosens his grip slightly, and I suck in air. "Dad—what if it's the police?" I rasp. "They might be trying to negotiate with you."

"I don't have anything to say to them."

Still, the phone keeps ringing.

"Well, how else are we going to get out of here?"

"I don't know!" Dad says, sounding desperate. His fingers tighten on the gun, and I know he's thinking about how easy it would be just to shoot me.

But I can't let myself think that way.

Dad's gut presses into me as he breathes. His eggy breath assaults my nose. I keep my body stiff, trying to block all feeling, but the rough hairs of his arm are against my jaw. I feel the warmth of his body and the beating of his heart, and it makes me want to vomit.

Mom's just sitting there crying, looking like a broken

toy. I can't believe I ever thought she'd protect me. I turn my head, try to breathe better. Here I am with both my parents, and neither of them really loves me. Not the way a parent should, anyway.

If I get out of here alive, I'm going to spend more time with the people who really care about me—Carolyn, Meghan, Sandy, even Mrs. Archer. I'm going to make *them* my family. At least I know they love me and would never want to hurt me—or sit passively by while someone else does.

My eyes begin to sting with tears. I want to be with the people I love, not pressed up against this man—this rapist—who's supposed to be my father.

The phone starts ringing again. As Dad pivots us around to face it, I know that this is it. I have to act right *now*—or I may not get another chance.

I grab Dad's arm and try to wrestle away his gun—even though I know it's the last thing I probably should do. But I just can't wait any longer—I can't stand being this close to him, can't stand knowing we might die any second.

"Mom, run!" I shout, as Dad's arm strains against mine, forcing the gun towards me. I feel him squeezing the trigger, then hear that deafening sound. The bullet rips into my shoulder, burning through my skin, and I scream.

Then Dad drops the gun, finally letting me go. He starts to cry. "I'm sorry, Kendra. I'm so sorry I hurt you."

Before he's even finished speaking, the front door bursts open and police officers charge in. They're all wearing visors and bullet-proof vests, and they have their rifles aimed at us.

"Get away from him," one shouts to me.

I stumble away and toward them, and they grab me, pulling me to safety. Dad raises his trembling hands in the air, looking terrified. I feel a kind of pity for him—but not compassion or love.

Now someone is tearing the sleeve off my shoulder and applying pressure, then taping on a bandage while talking softly to me: "It's only a surface wound; you're going to be okay." They wrap a blanket around Mom's and my shoulders, then lead us out of the house. They take Dad out, too—in handcuffs.

It's finally over. I know I should feel relief and happiness, maybe even sadness. But I don't. I can't feel anything at all, at least not yet. The only thing left is the numbness inside me.

Outside, the sidewalks are still wet from the rain, but the sun's shining so brightly that I have to squint to see. The crowd comes swarming toward us, shoving and trying to get past the police barrier. Cameras and lights mark our way, and reporters call out our names.

I'm shaking now and close to screaming as the police officer directs me toward the ambulance, guiding me by the arm. Then a good, familiar voice calls my name, and I turn.

It's Carolyn, waving to me from the front of the crowd. I stop, the policewoman stopping with me. "That's my therapist! I need to see her."

"You need to get checked out, first; you've just been shot," the officer says.

"What I need is my therapist." I say, clutching the blanket around my shoulders and shaking even harder.

The officer must see the panic in my eyes because she nods at the cop to let Carolyn through.

I run to her, and she hugs me close. "Kendra! Oh Kendra, I'm glad you're okay!"

"Carolyn. I'm so glad you're here," I say, laughing and crying at the same time. I lean into her, my shoulder throbbing, and Carolyn holds me tighter.

Then I glance back at the ambulance. There's Mom, sitting on the ambulance's rear step, talking to the paramedics, not once even glancing my way.

Carolyn rocks me, and I close my eyes, letting everything else float away. Carolyn might never be my mother, but she gives me so much more than Mom ever has. She gives me what I need. And that makes her my mother in my heart.

Carolyn holds my head and looks into my eyes. "I was so worried about you," she whispers.

"You called the police, didn't you?" I ask.

"After what you told me, and with your father so agitated at our meeting—and then I couldn't reach you on your cell or at home—I just didn't know what else to do!"

"You saved me," I say, squeezing her tight. "That's what you did!"

Carolyn kisses the top of my head. "From what I hear, you saved yourself."

"Kendra!" Meghan calls out.

I look around, not seeing her. Then I hear grunts and complaints in the crowd as people are jostled and shoved. Meghan elbows her way up close to where we're standing

"Please, could you—" I say to the officer, who looks

amused as she ushers Meghan through. Carolyn lets me go, and Meghan rushes to me, turning her back to the crowd. I open my arms and she holds me—so tight I can hardly breathe.

"I was coming over to find out why you weren't in school when I saw all the cops!" Meghan says. "God, Kendra—are you all right?" I feel her rapid heartbeat against me, her worry and love so strong. I kiss her gently, then turn to Carolyn for introductions. "Carolyn, this is Meghan. Meghan, Carolyn."

They shake hands and make some awkward small talk. I watch them, feeling almost high. I'm alive—and two of the people I care about most are right here beside me.

"Are you all right?" Meghan asks again.

"I am now."

39

"Kendra!" Mom calls from the ambulance. "They want to check you over."

I roll my eyes at Meghan and Carolyn, but Mom calls again, her voice shrill and insistent.

"I should get over there," I say.

Meghan moves closer to me. "I'm goin' along with you."

"I think that's a good idea," Carolyn says. She hesitates. "Would you like me to come, too?"

"Yes!" I say. "I mean—if you don't mind. I know it's weird, since we're not in session—"

"I'll make an exception this time," Carolyn says, smiling warmly. "It's important, and I want to be here for you."

I walk over to the ambulance, Meghan on one side, Carolyn on the other. I feel stronger and taller, just walking between the two of them.

I look over at Dad, hunched up, sitting in the back of the cop car. *You won't hurt any more kids now—not if I can help it.*

Dad raises his head, almost as if he hears my thoughts. I meet his gaze without flinching, and he looks away first.

A paramedic motions for me to take off the blanket, then pushes my flapping sleeve aside. He peers beneath the bandage as I stare up at the grey sky.

"I'm fine. You guys already took care of this."

"We just want to be sure. With a gunshot wound, we have to be careful that everything's all right. Do you feel any dizziness? Are you at all light–headed?"

"No—I'm fine."

"You didn't tell me you were shot!" Meghan cries, pressing her hands to her chest.

I start to laugh; I just can't help myself. Meghan and Carolyn are staring at me, then they're laughing, too.

"I don't see what you all have to laugh about," Mom says crossly. And that makes us laugh even harder.

Carolyn wipes the tears from her eyes. "Forgive me, Mrs. Marshall. Sometimes laughter is a good release in situations like this."

Mom frowns disapprovingly, but she looks a bit less offended.

Then the police officer who's been watching us adjusts her belt. "If you're both okay, we'd like to take you down to the station for questioning."

That pretty much quells my laughter.

"Is that really necessary right now?" Carolyn asks the police officer. "Kendra's just been through a major trauma—"

"Most folks find it easier to get it over with, rather than

have it looming," the policewoman says. "Besides, we're more likely to get something that will stick to the perp if we can get all the info while it's fresh in everyone's minds. The most I could give her is a few hours—but she wouldn't be able to talk with anyone during that time. We want to be sure we get her testimony, not anyone else's."

Carolyn rests her hand on my shoulder. "What do you think, Kendra? It's really up to you."

Mom purses her lips, but she doesn't say anything. She just leans her head back against the ambulance doors, and I wonder if they've given her a sedative.

"Can they come with me?" I ask, motioning toward Carolyn and Meghan.

The officer hooks her thumbs into her belt. "Were they with you when the incident occurred? Are the two of them actual witnesses?"

"No, but—"

"Then I'm afraid they can't go with you. This is strictly a police matter now."

I can't handle this. I need to cut. Need to cut so badly.

Carolyn squares her shoulders. "I'm Kendra's therapist. I had a session with Kendra first thing this morning, then a meeting with her and her parents, where I witnessed the offender's volatile behavior. I'm also the one who called you, and I'm sure I can help your case."

The officer starts to speak, but Carolyn just keeps right on talking. I almost want to laugh, seeing Carolyn steamroll over the officer. I've never seen her like this. It makes me feel protected. Safe.

"And furthermore, Kendra's mother is in no condition

to give her any kind of emotional support, and Kendra will surely need it after all she's been through. I'm prepared to be there for her and to forestall any possible problems—such as panic attacks or emotional outbursts." Winking at me, she goes on: "I'll cancel my morning clients so I can be with Kendra."

The officer unhooks her thumbs from her belt, looking like she knows she's met her match. "All right, I guess we can use your account of earlier events leading up to the incident."

"I'm her girlfriend," Meghan says, gripping my hand. "And I'm not letting her go without me."

The officer shakes her head. "I'm sorry, young lady, but you'll have to meet up with her later."

Meghan's fists ball up, and she looks like she might actually punch the cop.

"Hey, it's okay," I whisper. "Carolyn'll be there. Besides, I'll really need you later. I'll call you when we're done, 'kay?"

"Promise?" Meghan says.

"Promise."

We hug one more time, and the officer leads us to her squad car. Mom gets in beside her, and Carolyn and I get in the back.

I wave to Meghan as the car pulls away, until I can't see her any more. Then I turn to Carolyn. "Thank you. I don't know how to say it enough—but thank you for everything today."

"That's all right," Carolyn says. "I'm glad I could be here."

I lean my head against her shoulder, and she puts her arm around me all the way to the station.

❈

They let Carolyn sit in with me during the entire interview, through all the questioning. When the pain and fear get too bad, I just look over at her and somehow that gives me the strength to keep going.

The detective is gentle with me, backing off when the shame and terror choke my voice off or when the shadows rip through my mind. And always, Carolyn is there. "Are you willing to talk about this in court, in front of a jury?" the detective asks. "I won't lie to you; it's a difficult, wrenching process, and it's not set up to be kind to victims. Some witnesses even say it feels like being raped all over again. But I'll work to prepare you. I think you can do it; you're a very gutsy girl."

The detective looks at me over her glasses, her eyes intense. "If you're willing to testify in court, I think we can put your father away for a few years—and keep him from hurting anyone else."

That's what I want, what I've always wanted—to be safe and to make sure others are, too. I take a deep, shaky breath. "Okay."

"You sure? It won't be easy."

"I'm sure," I say firmly, and I mean it.

"Good," the detective says, making a note on her pad. Carolyn squeezes my hand. "I'm proud of you."

And so am I.

40

Carolyn checks her watch, her face scrunching up. "I really should get going."

"We're just about finished here," the detective assures her.

"It's okay, really," I say, and give Carolyn a hug.

Carolyn holds my arms, looking deep into my eyes. Reassured, she nods. "Call me if you need me," she says.

I watch her go, feeling a slight wrench, but I mostly feel okay. Because I know she's going to be part of my life for a long time.

Then I answer a few more questions for the detective.

"Well, I think that's it," she says, putting her notebook down. "You'll just have to wait for your mom. I have some work to do, but you're welcome to stay here in my office with me. If not, you can wait on the bench down the hall."

As nice as the detective's been, it's hard having a stranger probe into things that I've only ever told Carolyn and Meghan.

"Thanks—but the bench will be fine."

She smiles at me, showing she understands, then walks me down the hall.

As we pass a closed door, I hear Mom screaming and crying. Sounds like they didn't give her sedatives after all.

The detective glances at me and picks up her pace.

The wooden bench is deserted—just the way I want it. I'm done talking to people, at least for now.

"Can I get you anything?" the detective asks. "A soft drink, tea, or a sandwich?"

I shake my head no. *I just want to go home.* I sink onto the bench, exhausted.

"Your mom shouldn't be much longer." The detective smiles at me, we say good-bye, and she heads back to her office.

I sit and wait. Now that I'm alone, shadows start filling my brain. I tear at the skin around my fingernail.

Everyone's been kind to me, but I can't help feeling like I've done something wrong. Maybe it's because I'm sitting in a police station. Or maybe it's because Dad used to say they'd lock me up if they ever found out. Ha. He's the one who did something wrong.

I listen to the clicking of keyboards, the clatter of footsteps, the voices that rise and fall. And every time a siren wails, I tense up. I have to keep reminding myself that it's over. He can never hurt me again.

Twenty minutes pass, then a half hour. Then forty-five minutes. I start to feel uneasy and alone.

I wish I could call Carolyn and ask her to come back. But she's already given me so much, and I know I can get through this by myself. I can call her tomorrow—and every day until my session if I want. And maybe I will.

The detective comes back down the hall and sits on the bench beside me. She smooths out her skirt, then says, "Your mom will be out soon; she's just going over some last details."

More like she's still freaking out.

"You sure you don't want anything to eat? Food can be helpful after a shock like this."

I wrap my arms around myself, saying, "No, thanks. I'm okay."

"It'll get better, Kendra. I know it doesn't feel like it right now—but it will."

I smile at the detective and try to keep myself from crying again. My dad's going to be charged, all because of me—

No, not because of me. Because of what he *did.*

"I know it'll get better," I say. And even though I don't really know it, somehow I still believe it.

The detective pats my knee, then stands up. "You're a brave girl, Kendra," she says softly. "I wish there were more like you in the world."

"Thanks." I blink fast and she starts off down the hall. I turn away—and then I see Sandy striding toward me, his face tight and worried.

I stagger to my feet, and he opens his arms, pulling me into a hug. It was never Sandy—just my own jackass of a dad.

I lean into Sandy, breathing in his clay, soap, and cologne smell, and I feel myself finally relax. I'm so glad it wasn't him. So glad I know for sure now.

"Your mom called me," Sandy says in a choked voice. "I'm so sorry, Kendra. I should have realized—"

"How could you?" I say, pulling away so I can see his face. "I didn't even know it myself. I mean, I shoved it away so far and so deep, I didn't remember—"

Sandy smooths back my hair. "It was in your art, Kendra. Your abuser always in the shadows—I knew it meant you couldn't face who it was. I suspected it was somebody you knew, but I had no idea who. And your dad—he just comes off so well, I never suspected him. If only I'd made you talk about it sooner—"

I shake my head. "I don't think I was ready to face it before today. And you helped me to get there, Sandy. You and Carolyn, Meghan, and Mrs. Archer."

Sandy hugs me again, squeezing the breath out of me. "You two are coming to stay with me tonight. And I won't take no for an answer."

I raise one eyebrow. "My mom agreed?" I can hardly believe it.

"I already told her. She's pretty shaken by this whole thing, but if I know Lori, she'll be back on her feet in no time."

He looks at me steadily. "And you, my girl—you're going to thrive. I can just feel it. And I'm going to be right there with you."

"I know you will." And I'm so glad.

41

Mom parks in the driveway, and we sit here, staring at our house. I don't think either of us is ready to go in. It's only been a week, but already the place looks dark and abandoned, the yellow police tape flapping in the wind. It looks like a house where something awful happened, a house that's finally telling the truth about all those horrible nights. But something good happened here, too. Without meaning to, Dad gave me my freedom.

I unbuckle my seatbelt. It's not just Carolyn and Meghan, Sandy and Mrs. Archer who'll believe me now. Everyone who was here that night, everyone who reads the newspaper or watches the news will get a glimpse of what really went on here. Even Mr. Blair called; he'd known something was wrong, but he didn't suspect this. Now he knows. Everyone knows. And it's all because of Dad and his gun.

It's ironic. The man who was trying so hard to silence me was the one whose actions got our story out to the world. I know that's going to have an impact on me, but somehow I'm not afraid. And I'm not ashamed, either. I just feel a lightness now, like I can breathe easier. And I don't think that's going to go away.

Mom's been different since we talked to the police—quieter, calmer, more thoughtful—and I hope it's a good thing. I hope she's not going to fall apart on me now that we're back here. But if she does, I'll handle it. I know that I can.

"Come on, Mom," I say, lightly touching her arm. "We have to face it sometime."

Mom nods, and we climb the porch stairs together. I can hear the thud of police boots in my mind again and feel Dad's arm against my throat. I wonder if Mom's remembering it, too.

She trembles beside me, and I'm starting to wish I'd let Sandy come along instead of telling him we could handle this on our own. But I wanted to face the house and what happened here by myself. I wanted to know I could do it. We walk into the living room together.

"There's something I have to do by myself, Mom. It has nothing to do with blades, I promise."

"Okay," she says, and she doesn't try to stop me.

I walk down the hall to my room, floorboards creaking as I go. I look at the bed where he raped me and at the desk where I painted; the room was my prison and my sanctuary—that room without a door I could lock. The pain's like a broken bone inside me, dull and ever present. But it doesn't bring me to my knees.

I've got my blade with me. I know I can cut when I need to, and I'll probably cut again. But I don't need to; at least, I don't right now.

I take a deep breath, turn around, and walk back down the hall. I won't sleep in my room tonight. Maybe I never will again. I'll make up the bed in the guest room and take my stuff in there. And if I can't handle that, then I'll crash at Sandy's instead. I know I have a home with him whenever I want it or need it.

But I want to be able to handle this—to face all the secrets that were hidden inside me for such a long time. I don't want anything he did to me left locked away in my mind, waiting to ambush me. I want to face every last memory—when they come. Carolyn says too fast can be too much, so I'll definitely take it slow. But I won't push them away—not completely—not ever again.

I walk into the living room, and the images of what happened there come at me hard. I tremble as I switch on the lights and see the two bullet holes in the wall. I can feel the heat in my bandaged shoulder—see his face again, pleading with me to understand.

Mom's still standing where I left her. She turns to face me. "I know I should have stopped him. I should have protected you."

Yes, you should have.

"We're both alive, Mom. That's what's important."

"I'm so sorry I didn't do anything, Kendra."

I don't know whether she's talking about last week or all those years of Dad coming into my bedroom—but it doesn't really matter anymore. What counts is that she's acknowledging her part in what happened—something I never thought she'd do.

"It's over, Mom. It's all over, now."

But it isn't over, not really. I'll have more memories to face, more feelings I don't want to feel. But now I know who he is, and this time I won't be alone. And this time, I know I'll be safe.

"You're so much stronger than I am," Mom says.

I don't argue with her; it's true.

"I can never make it up to you, Kendra, but I want to try."

"All right," I say. *Make it up to me.*

❁

A week ago, hearing her say those words, I would've been angry and hopeful at the same time. But now I just feel detached, somehow separate from it all.

I've stopped hoping that Mom'll be the way I need her to be. I just don't think she can. In fact, I've given up expecting anything from her at all.

And though there's such sadness inside me, there's a lot of relief, too. Because I know who I can turn to whenever I need comforting, help, or love. I know it won't be Mom, and I'm actually okay with it now.

❁

"I've been thinking about going into therapy, myself," Mom says. "Carolyn's recommended some counselors for me."

I blink, surprised.

Mom twists her wedding ring, then yanks it off and throws it into the fireplace.

"I saw you blossom through therapy, Kendra. You really did. I saw you grow as soon as you had a little support. I was jealous that someone else could do that for you, especially because I couldn't. And I've decided it's time I took care of myself, so I can take better care of you."

I won't hold my breath. But if it happens, I won't turn her away.

"That's good, Mom—really good."

Mom smiles at me a bit crookedly. "I know I'm way behind you, but I'm going to try to catch up."

"I'm glad."

Mom's hand flutters at her throat. "There's something else I need to tell you. I called the bank the other day and then your father's workplace, too. It turns out he didn't lose his job. He'd cut back on his hours himself, told them he had a family emergency."

I stare at her, letting that news sink in.

It's hard to believe that Dad pretended to lose his job and told us all those lies just to follow me around. He worked hard at trying to keep me quiet; he must've panicked that I'd eventually remember who he was and talk about it. Well, he was right about that part.

I realize Mom's still talking, that I'd totally tuned her out.

She looks at me, her eyes watering. "He never even applied for a loan. The bank says our mortgage is in good shape—and there's more savings than I even knew about. So we don't have to move after all. Not unless you want to."

"I don't have to stop going to therapy? I don't have to

227

pull out of the art group, and I don't have to change schools?"

Or leave Meghan?

"No, Kendra. Definitely not."

My stomach twists, but this time, it's a good feeling.

I push her a little further. "And Meghan can come over whenever she wants? You'll make her feel welcome?"

Mom swallows. "I will." She touches my cheek. "And I promise I won't criticize your artwork, either—if you ever decide to show me anything else."

I almost can't believe her. I guess last week was life-altering for her, too.

"And you're okay with that?"

"I will be. I promise."

"Okay," I say. "Let's try it."

Mom throws her arms around me. "Oh, sweetie, I'm so relieved to hear you say that! I was afraid you were going to run away a few weeks ago."

"I was."

"It'll be different now, I promise. You'll see."

Yes, I'll see. If things get better between us, that'll be nice. But whether they do or not, it won't unbalance me. Because I've got my art to get me through; I've got people in my life who love me.

Happiness is just waiting for me to take it; I truly believe that now.

42

I stare out the window of the guest room at the pine tree that blocks our house from our neighbor's.

It's been nine months since we were on the news. And nine months that Dad's been sitting in prison, waiting for his trial to begin. They're going to charge him with rape and attempted murder. And if that last charge sticks, he'll do a lot more time than for the rapes, even though the rapes hurt me the most. But I don't care what he's charged with, as long as he can't hurt anyone ever again.

The prosecutor keeps saying how brave I am and how strong. And I guess I am, but I don't really see it that way. I'm just doing what I have to do.

Mom's supporting me on this, even now that she's had time to recover.

But I can't help wondering sometimes, if she'd be sitting there crying into her tissues in the prosecutor's office with me if Dad hadn't lost it that day—or if she'd still be in denial about everything he'd done. But I know she believes me, now, and that's something I'm grateful for.

❋

I'm starting to learn how to be happy for more than five minutes at a time and how to really hope and trust. And I'm finding out what it's like to sleep through an entire night without any nightmares.

I still have my bad days, when the memories press down on me like concrete, when they crush out all the joy—but those days are coming less and less often. Carolyn's been working with me to help me see that I can choose when to look at a memory and when to put it away.

She's also encouraging me to find other things I can do instead of cutting, and she keeps giving me steady support. I can feel myself changing—growing stronger. I've only cut a few times since Dad was put in jail. That's a miracle in my book.

I'll probably never know if I'd have been drawn to cutting if *he* hadn't taught me how to use it to keep me silent. I don't think it was always just me repeating the abuse or being under his control. My cutting was about trying to deal with more pain than I could handle. I've got other ways of dealing with it now, ways to pull myself out of it if I need to. And I have ways to get the comfort I need that don't come from the edge of a blade.

I catch myself staring at my arm sometimes, trying to figure out which scars were the first—the ones he made me cut. But I don't wonder for very long; I really don't want to know.

Other times, I look at my scars and see something else:

a girl who was trying to cope with something horrible that she should never have had to live through at all. My scars show pain and suffering, but they also show my will to survive. They're a part of my history that'll always be there.

And now, sometimes I don't bother hiding the scars. I just let them show, even though I get stares, rude comments, and questions from strangers. I figure I've already gone through the worst; getting stared at isn't that big of a deal.

I never want to have to keep anything else a secret, ever again.

❋

Mom knocks on the door frame of the guest room.

"Come in," I say.

"The woman from the Java Cup just called. She said two more of your paintings got sold—and you've had orders for three more. I guess you really have outgrown my help." She rubs her arms, looking surprised but proud, too. "You've got a style all of your own, Kendra, and it's clear that people like it. I'm glad I was wrong."

"Me, too. Thanks, Mom."

A few months ago, I would have thought she was criticizing me, and I probably would have been right. But now, I know that she's praising my work—in her own peculiar way.

I look around the guest room at my paintings hanging on the walls. I see the faces of Carolyn, Sandy, Meghan, and Mrs. Archer all smiling out at me, and for once, I don't hear Mom's voice in my head taking them apart with her criticism.

Instead, I hear Meghan's and Mrs. Archer's, and Carolyn's and Sandy's voices, each of them building me up, telling me how powerful my paintings are and how much my art moves people who see it. And I hear them all telling me how much I mean to each of them—and I know I'm loved.

"Dinner'll be in half an hour," Mom says. "You want to go out and tell Meghan, or shall I?"

"I'll tell her. Is she still in the backyard?"

"Yes." Mom laughs. "She's out there, talking to her plants."

I smile at this image. I've loved seeing Meghan take our huge, scruffy yard and turn it into a botanical paradise. I've loved seeing her find an outlet for her pain. I don't think it's that different from my artwork; it helps her get stuff out.

Mom turns to go and then stops. "And Kendra—thanks for giving me another chance. For trusting me."

"You helped me do that, Mom. You've worked at it."

And she has. Going into therapy was the best thing she could've done. It's not like all the tension between us has disappeared; it hasn't. But it's lighter now, not so loaded with resentment and anger.

I go out to the backyard, where Meghan's crouched over a clump of irises. She's talking softly to them. I move closer so I can hear.

"Come on, little flowers, you can do it. Keep on growing strong. I want to see you get there."

"Meghan?"

She turns to me, the sun on her face. "Hey, beautiful."

"Hey, yourself." I lean over to give her a kiss. "My mom's in a good mood today; I think we should ask about your staying over—permanently."

"I think we should, too."

I think Mom'll go along with it. She knows what Meghan has to live with at home. And I know she'll act as chaperone. I laugh at the thought, and Meghan grins at me, mussing up my hair.

We walk back to the house together, hand in hand.

Author's Note

I used to cut for many of the same reasons that Kendra did: to relieve unbearable emotional pain; to escape or suppress abuse memories and their related overwhelming emotions; to keep from killing myself; and to try to feel better. I also cut to silently cry out for help and sometimes to shut myself up or to punish myself.

And like Kendra, I cut because my abusers taught me to do it. This is a common occurrence in ritual abuse, though it isn't likely that it happens much outside of ritual abuse.

Like Kendra, I don't know if I would have turned to cutting as a form of coping if I hadn't been taught to do it. But I know that although cutting hurt me, it also helped me survive.

I also know that none of us deserves to be hurt, that it's important to treat ourselves gently, and that we need to surround ourselves with loving people who can mirror that love back to us. I hope you'll find ways to get support and comfort, to be gentle with yourself, and to take good care of yourself.

Resource Guide for Readers

There are many resources out there to help you—or someone you know—with self-harm, abuse, or homophobia. You can get free support through e-mail, phone, and support forums; and you can gain validating and helpful information through books, articles, and some websites. I think it helps to know that you're not alone—I know it helped me—and these sites and books can be ways to find that. Some information may be graphic or triggering, so, as with everything, please take gentle care of yourself as you look through the resources.

Websites
- Martinson, Deb. **Secret Shame: Self-Injury Information & Support.** http://selfharm.net

One of the best, most extensive websites on self-harm, written by someone who has self-harmed. This is the first place I'd go for information. It also has great sections for family and friends.

- Sutton, Jan. **Self-Injury and Related Issues (SIARI).** http://www.siari.co.uk

Lots of articles, links, and resources, including a support board for people who self-harm and a support group for helpers. Jan Sutton also provides detailed articles on self-harm that are excerpted from her books (*Healing the Hurt Within, Because I Hurt*).

- FirstSigns (Self-Injury Guidance and Network Support). **Self-Injury Awareness Day (SIAD).**
  http://www.firstsigns.org.uk/siad/

Self-Injury Awareness Day is on March 1, worldwide. This site includes a list of things you can do to increase awareness about self-harm, downloadable fact sheets and posters, an e-book on self-harm, a message board, a Facebook page, an e-newsletter, and more.

- **National Self Harm Network (NSHN).**
  http://www.nshn.co.uk/downloads.html

A great resource. The forum is active and the site provides PDF downloads that explain self-harm, provide do's and don't's for family and friends, suggest helpful distractions, and more.

- **Recover Your Life (RYL).**
  http://www.recoverourlife.com

Online self-harm support community that features articles, forums, chat and live help (twenty-four hours a day, seven days a week), and more.

- Mazelis, Ruta. **Healing Self Injury.** http://healingselfin jury.org

This blog by the editor of *The Cutting Edge* (a newsletter on self-harm that's no longer being published) provides information and articles about self-injury and houses past issues of *The Cutting Edge*.

- Martinson, Deb. **American Self-Harm Information Clearinghouse.** http://www.selfinjury.org

Lots of great info, some the same as at Secret Shame, but visually easier to read.

- **Self Injury Foundation.** http://www.selfinjuryfounda tion.org

This site has great information on self-harm, including a fantastic article on how crisis and hotline staff can respond in ways that are truly helpful to people who self-harm, an excellent question–and–answer section not just for people who self-harm but also for their parents, family members, and friends; and more. Self Injury Foundation is a non-profit organization. One of its goals is to obtain donations and grant money to develop a twenty-four hour crisis line for self-injurers.

- **Sidran Institute: Traumatic Stress Education and Advocacy**. http://www.sidran.org

Good information on trauma; PTSD (post-traumatic stress disorder); abuse; and coping mechanisms, including self-harm.

- **Survivorship.** http://www.survivorship.org

Great information and articles, and a newsletter for survivors of ritual abuse, mind control, and torture and their friends, families, and supporters. This site also offers webinars, links, and more.

- **S.M.A.R.T. (Stop Ritual Abuse and Mind Control Today)** http://ritualabuse.us

Tons of information on ritual abuse by an organization that works to stop ritual abuse and help survivors through education. The site offers online articles, a bimonthly newsletter, an e-mail discussion list, information on annual conferences, and transcripts of the conferences. Some information on this site may be triggering.

- **Ritual Abuse, Ritual Crime and Healing.** http://www.rainfo.org.

Information and resources for survivors, therapists, and others. This site has articles, links, and tips on what to do during flashbacks, as well as art and poetry created by survivors.

- **Persons Against Ritual Abuse-Torture.** http://www.ritualabusetorture.org

Lots of information, articles, and resources on ritual abuse and torture. This organization also conducts research on ritual abuse and torture, and engages in activism to help stop ritual abuse and torture. Some information on this site may be triggering.

- **Mosaic Minds.** http://www.mosaicminds.org

An online community for dissociative abuse survivors with dissociative identity disorder/multiple personality disorder (DID/MPD). Includes forums, articles, suggestions on keeping safe, and other resources.

- **Rainbow Hope.** http://www.rainbowhope.org/forums

A forum in which lesbian sexual abuse survivors can talk and connect with each other.

- **Youth Resource.**
  http://www.amplifyyourvoice.org/youthresource

Online peer educators, links to resources and hotlines, articles on body image and health, articles such as "Coming Out to Your Parents," "Questions to Think About," and more.

- **PinkBooks.** http://www.pinkbooks.com

An extensive bibliography of young adult books for gay and lesbian readers.

- **I'm Here. I'm Queer. What the Hell do I Read?**
  http://www.leewind.org

An extensive listing of over 200 children's and teen books with lesbian, gay, bisexual, transgender, and queer themes or characters, as well as links and reviews.

Helplines
United States
- **National Youth Crisis HotLine.** 1-800-448-4663
- **Rape, Abuse, and Incest National Network** (RAINN). http://www.rainn.org
  1-800-656-HOPE
- **The Trevor Project.** Crisis and suicide prevention support for lesbian, gay, bisexual, transgender, and questioning youth.
  http://www.thetrevorproject.org
  1-866-4-U-TREVOR (1-888-488-7386)
- **Gay, Lesbian, Bisexual, and Transgender National Help Center.** http://www.glnh.org/hot line/index.html
  1-888-843-4564
- **Suicide Help Line.** 1-800-SUICIDE
  (1-800-784-2433)
- **Boys Town.** http://www.boystown.org
  1-800-448-3000 (24/7, USA)
- **Youth America Hotline.**
  1-877-968-8454 (24/7)

- **S.A.F.E. Alternatives.** If you have questions about self-injury, you can phone 1-800-DONTCUT in the United States or e-mail info@selfinjury.com. This is not crisis support, but they will answer questions.

Canada:
- **KidsHelpPhone**.
  http://www.kidshelpphone.ca
  1-800-668-6868
- **Toronto Rape Crisis Center/ Multicultural Women Against Rape.**
  http://www.trccmwar.ca/index.html.
  416-597-8808
  E-mail: crisis@trccmwar.ca
  (M-F, 9:30am-5pm)
- **Lesbian, Gay, Bi, Trans Youthline**.
  http://www.youthline.ca
  1-800-268-9688
  E-mail: askus@youthline.ca

Worldwide:
- **Befrienders.** http://www.befrienders.org. Find support hotlines and organizations according to country.
- **TeenHelp.** http://forums.teenhelp.org. Online forums and support.
- **RAINN International Resources List**
  http://www.rainn.org/get-help/sexual-assault-and-rape-international-resources

E-mail or Online Crisis Support

- **Rape, Abuse, and Incest National Network. (RAINN).** National Sexual Assault Online Hotline—Live, anonymous chat for victims of sexual assault (whether their attack took place today or decades ago); spouses, family members, and partners of victims; and friends of victims. http://apps.rainn.org/ohl-bridge/
- **The Samaritans.**
  http://www.samaritans.org
  E-mail: jo@samaritans.org (24/7)
- **TeenHelp.** http://forums.teenhelp.org
- **Toronto Rape Crisis Centre/Multicultural Women Against Rape.**
  http://www.trccmwar.ca/index.html
  E-mail crisis@trccmwar.ca (M-F, 9:30am-5pm)
- **Gay, Lesbian, Bisexual, and Transgender National Help Center.**
  http://www.glnh.org
  E-mail: glnh@GLBTNationalHelpCenter.org

Books:

Strong, Marilee. *A Bright Red Scream: Self-Mutilation and the Language of Pain.* Virago Press, 2000. ISBN-10: 1860497543.

Sutton, Jan. *Healing the Hurt Within: Understand Self-injury and Self-harm, and Heal the Emotional Wounds.* 3rd Edition. How to Books, 2008. ISBN-10: 1845282264. An informative, sensitive book on self-harm.

Schmidt, Ulrike. *Life After Self-Harm: A Guide to the Future*. Brunner-Routledge, 2004. ISBN-10: 1583918426.

Alderman, Tracy. *The Scarred Soul: Understanding and Ending Self-Inflicted Violence*. New Harbinger Publications, 1997. ISBN-10: 1572240792.

Arnold, Lois, and Anne Magill. *The Self-harm Help Book*. Basement Project, 1998. ISBN-10: 1901335038. Booklet format, available at Amazon.co.uk.

Bass, Ellen, and Laura Davis. *The Courage to Heal: A Guide for Women Survivors of Child Sexual Abuse*. 4th Edition. Harper Paperbacks, 2008. ISBN-10: 0061284335. Very helpful, healing book for survivors of incest, sexual abuse, and ritual abuse.

Oksana, Chrystine. *Safe Passage to Healing: A Guide for Survivors of Ritual Abuse*. iUniverse, 2001. ISBN-10: 0595201008. Detailed, helpful, and validating book on ritual abuse.

Pia, Jacklyn M. *Multiple Personality Gift: A Workbook for You and Your Inside Family*. Ultramarine Publishing Company, 1991. ISBN-10: 0882478907. Excellent workbook with some great suggestions, reminders, and information on multiplicity and how to explore and communicate with parts inside.

Online Articles:

Martinson, Deb. "Bill of Rights for People Who Self-Harm." Secret Shame. http://www.selfinjury.org/docs/brights.html Fantastic bill of rights for everyone who self-harms.

Mollykat. "Things to Try to Keep Yourself Safe." http://www.geocities.com/mollykat1313/safety.html. An excellent, helpful page of suggestions for coping without cutting or self-harm. You can tell she's been there.

"Alternatives to Self-Injury." Secret Cutting and The Pain Behind Self Injury. http://www.angelfire.com/bc3/second-chance/alternativestosi.html. Tons of alternatives to help you avoid self-harm. Includes some excellent, practical, down-to-earth suggestions from someone who understands. (However, the support board is closed.)

Martinson, Deb. "Self-Injury: A Quick Guide to the Basics." Secret Shame. http://www.selfinjury.org/docs/factsht.html

Kharre. "Self Injury: Family and Friends. What Not to Say and Why." http://www.angelfire.com/or/kharreshome/page2.html. Great page about self-harm to give to friends and family; has an excellent section about what not to say and why.

National Self Harm Network. "Self-Injury: Myths and Common Sense." http://www.nshn.co.uk/facts.html

Martinson, Deb. "First Aid for Self-Injury." Secret Shame.
http://www.palace.net/~llama/psych/firstaid.html

Cutter, Deborah, Psy.D., Jaelline Jaffe, Ph.D., and Jeanne
Segal, Ph.D. "Self-Injury: Types, Causes, and Treatment."
HelpGuide.org. http://helpguide.org/mental/self_injury.htm

Alderman, Tracy, Ph.D., "Self-Inflicted Violence: Helping
Those Who Hurt Themselves." http://www.cyc-net.org/ref-
erence/refs-self-mutilation-alderman1.html. A good article
on self-harm for families and friends.

Rainfield, Cheryl. "What to Do When You Feel Like Hurting Yourself." CherylRainfield.com. http://www.cheryl-
rainfield.com/article_self-harm.html

"Famous Self-Injurers." Self-injury.net http://www.self-
injury.net/index.php?q=/media/famous-self-injurers

Sullivan, Kathleen. "Report of the Ritual Abuse Task Force,
Los Angeles County Commission for Women." Digital
Archive of Psychohistory. http://www.geocities.com/kid-
history/ra.htm. One of the best, most comprehensive defi-
nitions of ritual abuse. Goes into detail of various forms of
abuse, torture, and mind control that many cults use. Much
of the information in this article can be triggering.

Collings, Mari . "Reasons Not to Kill Yourself."
http://members.shaw.ca/pdg/reasons_not_to_kill_your-
self.html. A powerful, inspiring, healing poem on reasons

not to kill yourself, especially for survivors of ritual abuse and sexual abuse. You can purchase the beautiful poster from www.survivorship.org.

Additional Online Resources:

Self Injury: You Are Not the Only One
http://www.palace.net/~llama/psych/injury.html

Love Yourself: Joy–Filled Affirmations to Inspire, Encourage, and Comfort.
http://www.cherylrainfield.com/links.html

Video:

Broward County School Board. "Reality Avenue: Self Injury." http://www.youtube.com/watch?v=zHctN-NVSk8

Robinson, Jade. "Self-Harm BBC TV Interview."
http://www.youtube.com/watch?v=gPxj86oOifg